ROYAL

reckoning

D1557400

EMILY SILVER

TRAVELIN' HOOSIER BOOKS

For Tutu, a queen in her own right

A Note from the Author

Thank you so much for reading Royal Reckoning! I have taken some literary license when writing this book in regard to the royal world and the Succession to the Crown Act, passed in 2013. Prior to 2011, any second-born male could displace an older sister in line to the throne. Since this is my own royal world, this does not apply in this book.

Happy reading!

Chapter One

ELLIE

"**E**leanor, are you paying attention?"

The smack of papers in front of me pulls my attention away from the large windows of the palace. The London skies are a dull grey. A stern look from my advisor tells me that she has lost my attention, even though I heard every word she said. It's another endless cycle of luncheons, plays, and—

"Wait, what about the new after-school art programme?" It was a rare day when my granddad and I were to attend an event together. The new art school opening in Shoreditch was going to be the bright spot in my day.

"It's been pushed back. Not much detail was passed along, but I believe their funding fell through at the last hour. Now, after the luncheon and meeting with the Australian ambassador, you will have the new play opening tonight in the West End."

I should be used to the endless list of events, but it's frustrating that the one event I'm actually excited about gets canceled.

"You should enjoy the play. British history at its finest." Alice shows more enthusiasm about my events than I do. My eyes roll on their own at the thought of this new play I'll have to suffer through.

Her lips purse. "You will need to show more excitement when you show up."

My back straight as a steel rod, I take a sip of my now cool morning tea.

"British history has been drilled into my head since I was old enough to read. This is nothing I haven't heard before. Taking what wasn't ours, being kicked out. Battles. I will act appropriate for the event." I keep the sharp retort about being flayed by the paparazzi to myself, as they will no doubt be swarming the event this evening.

I give her a sharp eye, a sheepish look coming over her.

"Are you causing trouble in here?" The deep voice of my grandfather alleviates the annoyances of my morning.

"No more than you are." Smirking at him, I finish my tea and stand. Smoothing my hands down the plain fabric of my blue sheath dress, I walk over and give him a hug.

"Your Majesty." Everyone is quick to curtsy in front of the king.

"How are you this morning, Granddad?"

"Old. I hear that you and I no longer have our event today." The wrinkles in his old face cut deep.

"We don't. I was very much looking forward to spending the morning with you." I loop my arm through his as we walk out of my office.

"Shame. I always like the art programmes." Our pace is slow. He's more frail than someone his age should be. "What else is on the diary for the day, Wildflower?"

I smile at the familiar nickname. "Lunch with the Australian ambassador and then the new play opening tonight. I get to learn about British history in three hours this evening."

"Now, now." His hand claps down on top of mine where it's linked with his arm. "You may end up learning something."

"Okay, Granddad." I laugh at him as we turn into his private study. "I will be sure to let you know if I discover something new about us Brits."

"That's the spirit." His bones creak as he sits down into the old chair behind his ornate desk.

"And what will you do with your day now?"

"Might see your mum for lunch. We'll all be heading on holiday soon, so should see everyone while I still have time."

"No need to be so morose. It's not like you won't be around when the holidays are over."

"Forgive me, Eleanor. I just want to spend more time with those I love."

"Speaking of your favourites." The loud voice of my brother James carries through Granddad's office.

"No one said you were the favourite, Jamie." Life has always been easy for my twin brother. He was born seven minutes after me, forever sealing his fate as third in line to the British throne.

"I beg to differ. Morning, Granddad." He drops a kiss on his cheek before he comes to pull me out of my chair. "I need to borrow Ellie for a bit. I'll have her back before your big event today."

"It was canceled."

"Perfect. More time for me." I kiss my granddad goodbye as I trail behind Jamie, wondering what he wants with me.

"Sis. I'm so glad I caught you today." He pulls me close into his side as we make our way to his office through the gilded halls of the palace. The portraits of past kings and queens line the hall. Their regal stares are a stern reminder as to what will one day be my own legacy.

"What are your plans for this evening?" James is a mirror image of me, with dark hair and deep blue eyes, except where he is tall and lithe, I am shorter and curvier. Something the media never ceases to point out.

"I have the new play opening this evening." I help myself to another cup of tea as I make my way over to the plush red loveseat. Everything in the palace is ornate and over the top.

"Good heavens, you're not wearing that, are you?" His look of disgust is palpable.

"No, I was not planning on it. You don't have to be so horrified at what I'm wearing. This is only for the luncheon today."

"Sorry, Ellie. Came out wrong."

"I get enough grief from the media and my own people. I don't need you criticising me."

He holds his hands up in defeat as he sits next to me. "Sorry, you're right. Wanker move. But I am hoping you'll join me for an evening out."

"Did you not just hear what I said? I have the play opening tonight."

He waves me off like this is a minor inconvenience. James acts as if his whole life is one big party. "That's early. You haven't been out with us in ages. I want to head to Club Mayfair tonight, and you can't say no to me."

"And why's that?" I raise my eyebrows in his direction. It's very easy to say no to my brother. Most people don't because he is so persistent, but not me.

"Charlotte is going to be coming out with us." Damn. I haven't seen my cousin in a few weeks, and she's one of my favourite people. Not many people know what it's like to grow up under a microscope, but she is one of them. "Besides, I won't get in as much trouble if you come with me."

"I'm not your keeper, James."

"Ooh, James. Now I know I'm in trouble." His voice is full of laughter. Nothing ever fazes him.

I stand and walk over to the windows. Even in the grey, dreary day, the Royal Mall still stands proud in all her glory. "Can you ever just be serious for once?"

"My dear sister. You need to loosen up. Even Grandmum has a more exciting life than you. You need a little excitement in your life. Besides, how do you plan on finding a partner if you aren't going out and searching?"

"Sleeping with half of London isn't the same as finding someone to take on this life. Besides, you know it isn't the same for me as it is for you. You're the playboy prince, and I would be labeled a slut if I so much as looked at a man."

I hate the double standard of being a royal. Instead of enjoying life as a twenty-eight-year-old woman, I have to attend charity events and state dinners almost daily. My life has never belonged to me. It's been out for public consumption since the time my parents stepped foot outside the hospital wing when we were born.

"You look awfully sullen over there." Jamie pours himself a cup of tea, sitting in the chair opposite mine. "You need a night out. Please come, Ellie." His pleading brown eyes stare into mine.

"Fine. I'll go with you. You're lucky Charlotte is coming, otherwise you'd be on your own."

"Thank goodness! Who knows? Maybe you'll find a grumpy prince to match your own attitude."

"And maybe you'll find someone who has more than two pence to rub together." My snarky attitude is

5

unmatched today. My busy diary of events is weighing heavily on me, more so than usual.

"That's unfair. It's usually more like three."

Laughter bubbles out of me. My brother is one of the few people who knows how I truly feel about royal life. That on a good day, it's suffocating. That I can't take the pressure of being in the spotlight. Any weight gain or loss is scrutinized for days by the tabloids. It makes his criticism of me that much harder.

For leading such a privileged life, all I want are the simple things. Waking up, going to a job I love, and coming home to a small flat that I pay for. Instead, I'm shuffled between events, never alone, and coming home to an empty cottage that is more or less funded by taxpayer dollars.

There's a sharp knock on the door, followed by Alice entering. "Your Royal Highness, Princess Eleanor. In order to make it to the event on time to allow for a walkabout, we will need to leave promptly in ten minutes." Her voice is short and to the point. I stand, giving a sad smile to my brother.

"No rest for this royal. I'll see you later." He stands, giving me a quick hug.

"I promise, tonight you'll feel better. I'll make sure of it."

I follow Alice out the door. The history of the palace walls bears down on me as my Personal Protection Officers, my PPOs, follow behind me. Taking the wide stairs down, I find the black town car standing under the receiving entrance, ready to whisk me from event to event today. I sigh, settling in for an interminable day ahead.

———

"PRINCESS ELEANOR. It has been such a pleasure to have you join us this afternoon. We are honored that you could be with us for such a special occasion." The Australian ambassador shakes my hand whilst dipping into a low curtsy.

"The pleasure is all mine, madam." I give her a bright smile. "It's been quite some time since I've been to Australia. Hopefully I will get down there next year."

"I think I speak on behalf of all Australians, Your Highness, that we would welcome you with open arms."

"Australia is always a favourite of mine to visit." We're at the door, ready to leave, when I plaster on my press-ready smile.

"Thank you so much for visiting with us today."

I nod as I head out into the flashbulbs of the press. "Until we see each other again."

My PPOs are pushing the press back as we head towards the waiting car.

"Princess Eleanor! Why did you choose to visit with the Australian ambassador over Canada's?"

"Your Highness! Why did you go with such a scandalous outfit today?"

"Eleanor! Care to comment that you've gained a stone this last month?"

The door to the car swings open and I slide in. We're off in an instant as I try to drown out the comments from the press. Only one comment about my weight today. Usually, it's all they can focus on. The comments regarding what I wear are normally saved for after the evening event. Must be a slow news day.

"Your Highness. You'll have an hour for dinner and time to switch into your evening wear before we need to leave for the show tonight." Alice is focused on the tablet in front of her, not paying me any mind.

"Thank you, Alice." My eyes are on all the people waving as we leave the embassy behind us.

"And remember to wear the black dress this evening. It's more slimming and will hopefully ward off any unwanted comments from the paparazzi."

Just another day in the life of a princess.

Chapter Two

SEAN

"So for today's session, we're going to outline everything, and then once it heals, you'll come back in a few weeks for the colour."

"Sounds great, man. Let's get rolling." Looking down at the intricate pattern before me, it's hard to contain my excitement at my latest piece. The level of detail even blew me away. It's an old-time maritime scene, complete with wooden boats, pirates, and sailors. Once the colour gets added in, it's going to be fucking amazing.

My station prepped and ready, I get to work. The buzzing of the tattoo gun is a balm to anything going on in my life. It's been a stressful few weeks, but whenever I'm working on someone, the background noise fades away. I love watching the way the ink bleeds into the skin to create a masterpiece.

"So how long have you been doing this?" Wiping the excess ink off, I grab more and keep moving on the lines of the boat.

"'Bout ten years now."

"You been in Shoreditch for a while?" he asks. I don't

mind the idle chitchat that people make when getting tattoos. It usually helps distract them from the pain.

"Best spot in London."

"Oy, Sean! Call for you." Trevor's voice carries over the shop, distracting me from my work at hand.

"Sorry, mate. Be right back." Pulling the gloves off, I grab the phone from Trevor.

"Sean speaking."

"Hi, Sean. It's Melanie."

"Melanie. Where the hell are you?" It's the first time I've noticed she hasn't been in the shop all morning. She's usually the first one here out of all of us.

"Listen, I'm sorry to do this over the phone, but I can't work there anymore." Her voice is quiet as she drops the news on me.

"What do you mean you can't work here anymore?" I can't hide the irritation in my voice. Instead of working on the piece I've been looking forward to, I'm having to deal with this kind of shite.

"It just isn't going to work out. I'm so sorry." She ends the call, leaving me hanging.

Fucking hell.

"Pierce! What the hell happened?" I can't contain the annoyance in my voice when my brother appears in front of me.

"What happened about what, bro?" Crossing his arms, he leans against the wall, looking calm and collected, the exact opposite of how I feel.

"You know what. Why did I get a call that our receptionist quit on us?" This is the third one we've lost this month.

"It's probably because she asked out Trevor and he said no. You know how everyone is about him." He rolls his eyes. I do know, and it's a pain in my arse. Every person, man or woman, has fallen at his feet when they start working here. If he wasn't so damn good at his job, I'd think twice about keeping him on.

"We need a no fraternization policy amongst the staff. I can't keep hiring for this bloody job." Even though Trevor has been with his girlfriend for a number of years now, it doesn't stop anyone from asking him out.

Scrubbing my hands over my stubbled jaw, I know this day just got infinitely longer. Owning my own tattoo parlour, the responsibilities fall to me. I could pass them off to my brother, but sometimes his whining could do me in.

"Sean, relax. It's going to be fine. I've got a slow day if you need me to help out." I hate that word. Relax. Did anyone in the history of the world ever relax when someone told them to relax?

"I'm going to go get a jump on my day so you don't throttle me. Let me know if you need my help." Pierce leaves me be, whistling, just to irritate me further. Some days, I love working with my brother. Other days, like today, I could strangle him. I have enough on my plate to worry about other than to take walk-ins and calls about design work.

Thankfully, the rest of my day should be relatively easy. The piece I'm working on now should only take a few hours, and after that, my schedule is light.

Dropping the phone, I grab a new set of gloves and get back to work. "Sorry about that, mate."

"No worries. Can't imagine having to deal with people and their crap."

I just shake my head. "Tell me about it."

I love my job. I really do. I love seeing the pieces people dream up come to life. I started out like any other tattooist, doing butterflies and Chinese characters that people wished to mean hope and joy. But after graduating from uni with a degree in art and design, I started working my way up and opened my own shop. I love getting to mentor the people who are just starting out and nurture their talent. It makes me feel like a proud parent when their work is done.

It more than makes up for the annoyances I'll face in having to hire someone new. I was able to nab a prime piece of real estate on the high street here in Shoreditch. It usually equates to a lot of walk-ins for business, but also, a higher probability that I'll be able to fill Melanie's spot soon.

"Sorry about the last girl, mate." Trevor's voice is loud against the noise of the shop. "Hopefully we'll find someone soon."

"Maybe if you put a paper bag over your head while working, we might have a better time keeping someone around," I joke. Trevor and I have worked together since our apprenticeship, and we've become mates because of it.

"Or maybe I should tattoo my girlfriend's face on my arm." He cringes at the thought.

"You know the rules. No faces or names."

"Don't I know it." I did a cover-up for him a few months back on an old girlfriend's name. It's my shop rule —no names or faces of people that aren't permanent in your life. I could retire off the number of people who come back for cover-ups because they regret it later.

"Maybe just put a picture of you two up together to ward off the crazies."

"Yeah, I don't think that'll turn people off of you." The guy in the chair that he's working on pipes up with his two cents.

"Oy! Don't add to his already huge ego. He already has a hard enough time fitting it in the door."

"What can I say, Seany, people love a bad boy." As if to

prove his point, he flexes his arms. If he wasn't working on someone, I'd throw something at him.

"Feck off, and get back to work."

"Excuse me, hi. I was hoping to talk to someone about a new tattoo?" A quiet voice pulls my attention away from Trevor.

Pierce gives her his winningest smile, welcoming her in. "Sure, follow me."

———

THE NOISE of the pub is deafening. I couldn't handle a quiet night at home, so I dragged the boys out after work.

"You know it's a bad day when Seany is the one dragging us out." Pierce winks at me as he uses my childhood nickname.

"Feck off. It's been a bloody rotten few weeks, and now I have to deal with hiring someone new."

"Just hire Trevor's girlfriend. Then you won't have to worry about anyone hitting on him."

"Tough luck, mate. Ruby wouldn't leave her school for anything. Even for me." He glazes over at the mere mention of his girlfriend. What a sucker.

"Smart girl," Pierce quips.

"Look, I don't care who we hire, as long as we hire them quickly. Because we'll be rotating who takes the walk-ins now." Both of them groan before diving back into their pints.

"Quit your bloody whining." I shake my head as I go back into my own.

"You really need to get laid, bro." Not with this shit again.

"I don't need to get laid. I'm doing just fine," I say while flipping him off.

"I agree with Pierce. So you know it must be bad," Trevor agrees.

I brought the lads out tonight because I needed the distraction. I didn't want to be on the receiving end of their jabs.

"You think we could find him someone to take home?" Pierce's eyes are now roving around the bar.

"Fecking hell. There is no way I'm taking home some random woman tonight."

"Sheesh. We're just looking out for you. You really do need to lighten up."

"You two are buying the next round for all your talk." They both shrug their shoulders at me and go back to their perusal of the women at the bar.

While I know what they are saying is true, I don't want to worry about a girlfriend right now. After everything went south with the programme I wanted to start, I couldn't focus on anything but the shop.

And the shop is my life. It's what I've always wanted in my life. From tattooing myself, to my very first anchor tattoo that I inked on another person, I was hooked. So much so that I have that same tattoo on my bicep. It's a reminder of how far I've come, but also where I still want to go in life.

"As much fun as it is razzing you, Sean, I'd rather be home with my girl." Trevor has never been happier than when he is with Ruby. I can't fault him for wanting to be at home with her, rather than keeping us company.

"Piss off, mate." Pierce is oh so kind in his dismissal of him. Trevor flips him off as he drops a few pounds on the table.

"See you boys for Sunday lunch." They've become a second family to us since we opened our own shop. It's what helps pass the days when I can only focus on keeping my shop above water.

"Of course we'll be there. We wouldn't want to get on Ruby's bad side." He claps me on the shoulder as he heads out of the pub.

"As much as you're content with your life over there, Sean, I'm going to go and find me a lady for the evening."

"Godspeed."

Chapter Three

ELLIE

I should've known better. Jamie said he would make my coming out tonight worth my while. We hadn't even gotten our drinks before he was distracted by a blonde, his "future queen" as he told me, and left me to my own devices. If only I had gone to Charlotte's beforehand, I wouldn't be sitting here by myself looking like a helpless little princess.

"Ooh, if it isn't the princess herself." I look up from where I'm sitting in the VIP section to see a tall, dark, and decidedly unhandsome man in front of me.

Looking around, I see my PPOs are stationed off to the side. Close enough in case there is a problem, but just far enough away to give me the illusion of freedom.

"Looking for your Prince Charming? He's right here." He waves his hands over himself before taking the seat right next to me. He smells of cheap cologne and bad vodka.

"I'll be sure to let you know if I find said Prince Charming." I slowly sip my drink, showing as little interest as possible. Usually, the whole princess thing is enough to scare any potential love interests off, but this man has a cocky air about him. He has no interest in me as a person. People like him only want to say they spent the night with the princess.

"Ouch. Right through the heart." His calculated gaze peruses my dark, form-fitting jeans and off-the-shoulder top. "Let me buy you a drink, then I can show you what a real Prince Charming I can be."

Who is this guy and where did he come from? I down the rest of my drink as the waiter brings over another. "Wow, they have great service here," he comments.

"It's been nice chatting with you, but I must ask you to leave now." It hasn't been nice chatting with him, and the longer he sits here, the more irritated I get.

"Oh, come off it. One drink, and if I can't show you a happily ever after, then I'll go."

A prince charming thinking he can show me a happily ever after? It's the most common pickup line I hear. And so dreadfully unoriginal.

"I'll pass." Looking around, I see Charlotte has finally arrived. Her timing couldn't be more impeccable.

"One more thing, Princess." I turn to look at him and he snaps a photo before I can even process what he's doing. As soon as the flash goes off, my PPOs are escorting him out of the VIP area as Charlotte squeezes her way in.

"Already getting into trouble, I see?" Charlotte asks, sitting next to me.

"Just someone who thought he was my Prince Charming."

Charlotte's face turns in disgust. "Ack, no thank you! Don't they know that is the most unoriginal thing we've ever heard?"

"Apparently every man thinks we'll fall at their feet at the mere mention of Prince Charming."

"I'd rather have a tattooed version of Jamie from Outlander." She wiggles her eyebrows at her latest obsession.

"You know, you could just call him up and have him at your disposal. A royal perk if you will."

"I like the way you think, Ellie." She looks around the club, as if trying to find someone. "Now, how did Jamie convince you to come out this evening?"

Being fifth in line to the throne, there is not as much pressure on her. Her schedule is lighter, and she handles the paparazzi with more grace than I do. Charlotte has always been a stunner. Curves she flaunts to the media, long dark hair that is expertly curled, and lips painted her signature dark red. She's a media darling.

I sip on my seltzer and vodka, the loud music in the club giving me a headache. "What can I say, Jamie made a good case tonight." My emotions are also on a trigger after a long day of events and comments about my appearance. "And it's been ages since I've seen you."

"We really don't see each other as often as we should. I'm pleased he managed to draw you out of the palace." Charlotte reaches over and squeezes my hand.

"Well, we're here tonight." Charlotte is one of my closest friends as she is one of the very few people who know what we go through. "Although, I will not be in charge of Jamie."

Jamie is a big fan of Club Mayfair and the attention of the women here. While I usually don't enjoy coming out, I needed it after my day. A lady can only brush off the comments of her appearance so often. Everyone tells me I should have a thicker skin, but it's hard. It's hard when everything you do is picked apart.

"No one should be in charge of James," Charlotte snickers over her own drink. He's currently dancing with a new woman. I can't keep track of the number of women he has had on his arm just tonight. It changes by the half hour. If I had a new man as often as he had a new woman, I would be labeled a slut by the paparazzi. Jamie is seen as the darling prince of the media who is only sowing his oats. The double standard is never-ending.

"Earth to Ellie. Are you even listening to me?" Charlotte pulls me out of my thoughts.

"Sorry, Lottie. Just been a long day for me." I sigh and gulp down the rest of my drink. Another appears before me. It's one perk of the VIP section—my hand is never devoid of a drink.

"The media is just terrible to you. You looked absolutely fab today, love." Switching my drinks, I give her a doubtful look.

"I thought so too. But apparently blue is not my colour."

"Well, I think you looked ravishing. If you don't want that dress anymore, I will gladly take it off your hands."

I give an unladylike snort into my drink. "And I'm sure you'll get rave reviews if you wear it. Might even find yourself a new man."

"I am not interested in finding another man. Not after Michael."

Charlotte's face still holds a sadness I wish I could wipe away. The press is awful to anyone we try to bring into our fold. Charlotte and Michael were together for two years before they broke up. Michael couldn't handle the scrutiny. Charlotte was devastated when their relationship ended. She thought he would be the one to finally stick.

Neither of us has ever had luck in the love department. As second in line to the throne, I know it will take a certain someone to fit into the fold. The few men I've dated were overgrown man boys and weren't worth my time. If only I could find someone who was worth it.

"Well, maybe you could have a little fun," I urge her. "Jamie can't be the only one out living his life."

"That's pretty rich coming from you." She gives me a knowing look. "When was the last time you did anything for yourself?"

"Maybe if my every move wasn't monitored, I would be able to. Thankfully my holiday is coming up, so maybe I'll be able to have some time for me."

Charlotte snorts into her drink. "A palace-approved holiday is the furthest thing from fun"

"I'll have you know I do love Kenya. It's always peaceful when I visit."

"Oh, please. You don't need to feed me that line. I know you'll be sucked into some sort of volunteer work while you're there."

I sigh, knowing it's true. There's no such thing as time off for a royal. "At least I won't have the media hounding me. That will be a nice break."

"A nice break would be a holiday from your life." It's a lovely idea, one that plants a small seed in my mind. Before I go wild with the idea, a sweaty Jamie plops down next to me, stealing what's left of my drink.

"And where is your flavour of the hour?" I give him a stern look.

"Lighten up, El. We're just having fun." As of late, I've been getting more and more irritated with my brother and his carefree attitude.

"Ah, yes. The playboy prince who can do no wrong."

"It's not my fault everyone loves me." Jamie flashes his most winning smile at me.

"Then maybe *you* should become king." Crossing my arms, I level him with a stare that is not to be messed with.

"Alright. I don't know why you have your knickers all twisted up about it. Power. Control. Women. It'll be bloody brilliant."

Of course he would think that of being second in line to the throne. Whereas I've spent my entire life learning from my granddad and mum, he's been allowed to do as he pleases. Go to the university of his choosing. Even do active military service in the Middle East.

"You are so not ready to be king, Jamie. You would fall flat on your arse!" Charlotte's voice carries over the noise of the club.

"But I would have a pretty woman at my side to help."

"Is that really all you think about?" Disgust is laced through my voice.

He gives me a dumbfounded look. "We're twenty-eight. What else would I be thinking about?"

"And on that note, I'm going to call it an evening."

"Come off it. You've barely been out with me in weeks. Don't you want to stay and hang out with your favourite brother?" Jamie gives me his best puppy dog eyes.

"So I can sit here and have a drink while you run off to find your next conquest?" Patting him on the cheek, I grab my purse and head over to Charlotte. "I'll see you later this week, Jamie. Charlotte, good luck with this one." I point behind my shoulder as I make my way through the noisy club. A few club-goers try to get my attention as I leave, but I make a quick getaway to the back exit.

My PPOs are ahead of me, ready to usher me out. "We've got a few paparazzi outside, Your Highness." Bloody hell. This was the reason I hated coming out. As the door is pushed open in front of me, I'm met with a wall of blinding light.

"Your Highness! Over here!"

"How are you responding to the reports about your recent weight gain?"

"Your Highness! Is it true you're seeing Tom Hiddleston?"

The door to the Range Rover is already open as I dive my way across the back seat. The slamming of the door cuts the noise to a dull roar in my head. The paparazzi are getting worse and worse as of late, commenting on the way I look, whom I'm dating, or any other scandal they deem worthy to drag me through the muck.

The worst is their comments on my appearance. No matter what good I do in the world, it will always be over-shadowed by whether or not I've gained a stone in the last month. My head aches as all of their shouted words fight for control.

As the car starts to pull away, I shift back to Charlotte's earlier thoughts. I'm supposed to be going on holiday for a few weeks, but what if I changed my plans entirely? What if I decided to be…*not royal?*

I was born into this life, my entire future planned out for me before I even knew my name. I still remember my panic as a little girl when a camera was first thrust in my face.

I never wanted to be a princess. It sounds terrible to say when I don't have to worry about a thing in my life, but I'm not built to be a princess. The constant attention on me is too much to bear. And I'm not even first in line to the throne yet. It will only get worse as time goes on.

But what if I could escape life, just for a little while? Where there were no expectations placed on me? No diary of events demanding my attention day in and day out? Maybe this upcoming holiday to Kenya will help me find more balance in my life. Or it might just be the perfect chance for escape.

Chapter Four

ELLIE

"When you arrive in Kenya, you will have a luncheon with the British ambassador followed by dinner with the president. The following day we'll have a selection of volunteer opportunities from which you can choose."

Alice is reviewing my itinerary with me for my supposed holiday. Instead of a relaxing few weeks, I am now looking at a packed schedule.

"Alice, do I have any time to actually take a holiday?" My voice is curt.

"Yes, Your Highness. If you see on page five, you have three days at the end of the month there. There are a few locations we've preapproved for the remainder of your time in country."

Three days in what should have been a month-long holiday. Charlotte's words echo around my head. *I know you'll be sucked into some sort of volunteer work while you're there.* By giving me options, they think it'll soften the blow of not having a proper holiday. I was hoping for a few weeks at the beach with nothing but a sinfully steamy romance novel to read and some time to get a better perspective on royal life.

Other than a royal tour scheduled at the end of the year through Canada, this would be my only time away from the palace. The weight of my schedule settles heavy in my chest.

"Alice, can we please continue this tomorrow? I'm feeling dreadfully tired."

"But Your Highness, you leave the day after tomorrow. We must review everything."

"There will be plenty of time tomorrow then. Now, if you'll excuse me." I stand, not bothering to listen to her objections as I leave the office in my cottage and head to my private quarters.

The gaudiness of my own bedroom isn't a reprieve from my spiraling thoughts. Heavy, velvet curtains hang from the floor-to-ceiling windows that overlook the sunken gardens around the palace grounds.

Flowers are dancing in the light breeze of the early evening. The chaotic noise of London is softer in this part of the grounds. Trying to pull myself from my sour mood, I head into my bathroom to draw a bath. The lavender bath salts I drop in are a balm to my frayed nerves.

Stripping out of my clothes, my gaze is drawn to my reflection in the ornate mirror. The bright lights do nothing to soften the harsh thoughts as I appraise my own appearance. By normal standards, no one would pay the slightest attention to the way I look. But being in the royal spotlight, every curve, every dip, and every new pound gained is highlighted and dissected for public consumption. And I detest it with every fibre of my being.

I've always been curvier. Heaven forbid a lady have some curves. I have my grandmum to thank for that. No matter how well I eat or how much I exercise, my thighs will always touch and my stomach will never be flat.

Turning the water off, I step into the tub and let the hot water invade my senses. Goose pimples erupt over my skin, the cold air surrounding me a contrast to the warm heaven of the water. It reminds me of the ocean waters off the Kenyan coast where I was going to be spending my holiday.

There has to be another way to actually get a holiday. More than just three days spent surrounded by my Personal Protection Officers. I don't want to worry about the foreign press snapping an unflattering photo of me and it making world headlines. The one benefit to a royal holiday is that I'll have Alice and one other advisor with me. It wouldn't be hard to make a change of plans once I get to the country. It might take some convincing, but it's worth the fight.

I hate that I feel this way. I hate that I can't brush off the criticism of the press and put a happy face on for my country. But mostly, I hate that I can't step away from my life, for even a few weeks.

My thoughts are pulled away when there's a rustling of noise outside my door before Alice barges into my bathroom.

"Alice! What on earth are you doing in here? Please leave at once!" I try to cover myself as best I can, but others are standing just outside the door. There is no such thing as privacy when you're a princess.

"I'm sorry, Your Highness, but please get dressed and come outside to speak with me. It's imperative." She drops into a curtsy as she leaves the bathroom, closing the door behind her.

Bloody hell. I can only imagine what is going on right

now for her to interrupt me. I can't even go thirty minutes without something requiring my attention.

Stepping out of the warmth of my bath, I dry off and slip into my satin robe. Piling my hair on top of my head, I step into my bedroom. Alice, two of my advisors, and my PPOs are all wearing looks of horror. This can't be good.

"What's going on that has you all looking like the world is ending?" Apparently that was a poor choice of words, as all their faces drop.

"Your Highness. Do you recall going out with someone and not having them sign an NDA?" Alice's face is trying not to be accusatory, but it's written clear as day over her expression.

"You know I haven't been out with anyone for ages. What's the meaning of this?"

"We received word that there is going to be a story in the press tomorrow from a man detailing his night with the princess."

I rear back, as if I've been slapped. "That's ridiculous. You know I haven't seen anyone in months." Alice keeps track of these types of things better than anyone I know. It's embarrassing to have to worry about, but it comes with the territory.

"Well, apparently this man has intimate knowledge of a night you two spent together this past week."

I start to protest when Alice turns and shows me the photo Prince Charming snapped before he was shown out of the VIP section.

"I'm sorry, but how does this insinuate that we spent a night together?" Whereas before I was trying to calm down, I'm now boiling with anger. "How was this picture not deleted?" I turn to my officers, no doubt an accusatory look painted on my face.

"It must have been on the cloud, Your Highness. We apologize for the oversight."

"You apologize for the oversight," I huff. "Now on top of having to go on a 'non-holiday holiday'"—my tone is coming out laced with anger as I wave my fingers in air quotes—"we'll have to deal with fallout from someone lying about having an intimate relationship with me."

"This kind of stuff happens with Prince James all the time. It will all blow over," Alice says quietly.

"And do you know why it blows over, Alice?" My rage is exploding out of me. After the long week I've had, it's the final tipping point. "It blows over because he's a man and they think it's endearing that Prince James loves all the women of his kingdom. It will not, however, blow over for me because I'm a woman. And as such, I'm held to a higher standard. An impossible standard when you add in the crown!" I'm shouting now. Everyone has backed up a few paces from me, but I can't keep my voice down.

"Everyone leave! I'm sure you will handle this without me needing to be present, seeing as how I haven't spent more than a moment's time with this despicable man. Out! Now!" I rush to my door and hold it open until everyone vacates my room. Slamming it shut, I stalk over to my bed and throw myself on top of it.

With everything else piled on top of me, I now also have to deal with a potential sex scandal. I'm always careful how I present myself, and because of one careless mistake by my PPOs, my carefully constructed persona I present to the world could be shredded with one photo.

With that horrid thought in my head, my determination takes hold. Come hell or high water, I will be having a holiday. A true holiday where I have no appearances to make, and where no one will even know I'm a princess. And I can't bloody wait.

———

I CAN'T REMEMBER the last time that I was so happy to see the hustle and bustle of a busy London morning. By this time in the morning, I would usually be off to my first event of the day. But instead of leaving for my spring holiday, I made a break for it.

Charlotte planted the idea, and the events of the other night made my decision an easy one. A holiday is never a true holiday as a royal. I always have to be dressed just right in case the media happen to find where I'm staying.

But right now, not a soul has paid any attention to the girl with pink hair. I was able to convince my PPOs to take me to the corner market by the palace, where no one pays me any mind late at night, and get a few things I needed to make my escape with no one noticing. Not even the paparazzi noticed, which is a feat unto itself.

And so, during the morning switchover of guards surrounding the palace, I ran. I packed a bag, left a note, and made my escape. Wanting to get as far away from the palace as possible, I came to Shoreditch. It was on my mind from our canceled event earlier this week, and with my new pink hair, I blend in perfectly with the artsy neighbourhood.

This cute, corner coffee shop has been the perfect start to my morning. The sun breaks through the grey clouds for a brief moment, warming my pale, winter-weary skin.

"Another cuppa?" The waitress comes by and I give her a quick nod. She barely gives me a second glance as she's off to the next table. It feels like there is a flashing sign above my head shouting *Runaway Princess! Call the palace at once! Do not let her escape!* But a woman with pink hair and large, oversized sunglasses? No one would believe it's the princess escaping her royal duties.

Sitting here, in the noise of London's rush hour, is a freeing feeling. To not to have a single moment of my day planned. I could do anything I want. I could spend all day sitting here in the café. I could wander through the main road here and shop in any store I want. It truly feels like the world is at my fingertips. Or, at the very least, the best of London.

Thanking the waitress for the second cup of tea, I notice a small shop across the street. A flashing, neon tattoo sign hangs above the door, but it doesn't hide the large 'Help Wanted' advert in the window. Maybe this would be the perfect way to spend the next few weeks. After all, my holiday was supposed to last about a month. Maybe I could get a taste of the life I've always wanted.

Fishing out my wallet, thankful I had the foresight to bring the cash I had on hand, I drop a few pounds on the table and gather the courage to ask for what I want.

———

"SORRY, we're not open for another hour." A deep voice rings out over the tinkling of the bells as I enter the tattoo parlour. Old Edison bulbs gleam off black and white chequed floors. Large posters of art decorate the space over separate stations.

"I was hoping to inquire about the 'Help Wanted' sign." The man behind the voice comes out of a small office behind the desk. My heart squeezes in my chest as I stare into the deep, navy-blue eyes of the sexiest man I've ever laid eyes on.

A sleeve of tattoos decorates one arm, and the muscles in his arms flex as he stares me down. Brown hair hangs over his eyes as his gaze moves over me, leaving zings of electricity in its wake.

"Do you have any experience with being a reception-ist?" His face gives nothing away as he stares me down.

"Yes, I do. I am highly organized and can deal with all types of people." Not a lie. Even though Alice always manages my events, I can tell you what is on the diary for the next few weeks at any given point. And I've gotten very good at the princess smile. I can fake it with the best of them.

"Do you have your documents?"

Shite. This might be over before it even starts. "Look, I don't have them with me." Think, Ellie, think. "I left in quite a hurry and was only able to grab a few things. I could really use this job."

The mystery man in front of me scrubs a hand down his face as he takes me in. "Look, you have to have proper documents to work. I can't get around it. But if you need work for a few weeks, I can help you out until I find someone permanent." His gaze softens a bit.

"That's all I need." I reach forward, resting my hand on his arm. He jumps back, as if on fire. But I felt it. The spark that practically leapt between the two of us at the briefest of touches.

"Alright, welcome to Shoreditch Ink." He turns to go, but I stop him.

"Sorry, what's your name?"

"Sean. Sean Davies." He doesn't extend a hand, as if he's afraid I might burn him with a simple handshake. "And you are?"

Bollocks. I can't give him my real name. What if he puts two and two together? "Kat. It's Kat." Again, not a total lie. My middle name is Katherine after all.

"Alright, Kat. Let's get started."

———

"OKAY, so here is the reservation system. Bookings are over here, and inquiries are over here where you need to call them and get more information as to what they want." It's hard to focus with Sean leaning so close to me. His clean laundry smell invades my senses.

"Reservation system. Got it." It can't be that hard, can it?

"Are you paying attention?" He pulls back from where I'm sitting and crosses his arms. Thick, corded forearms flex under the tattoos inked along his skin on one arm. I have never felt so drawn to another person before. I thought earlier might have been an adrenaline high from absconding on my holiday. But it's not. It takes all my willpower to not reach out and trace the lines of his tattoos with my fingers.

Snapping fingers in front of my vision startle me out of my ogling. "If you can't pay attention, you can go." Sean's deep voice is annoyed. Not wanting to be let go, I turn back to the computer and show Sean exactly what he told me. I may be distracted, but I can still figure out a computer. It's one thing I've perfected over the years— drifting off while Alice goes over my diary in painful amounts of detail but still retaining everything she says.

"Fine. You were paying attention." His jaw ticks, as if it annoys him that I might be good at this job. "If you have any questions, let me know."

He stalks over towards his station, growling as he goes. My eyes are drawn to him as he walks away. The way the black T-shirt pulls taut over his back. The way his jeans hug his backside just right.

"See something you like?" I jump at the sound of a voice next to me. Sean's brother, Pierce, is grinning like a Cheshire cat. Sean begrudgingly introduced him to me earlier. My face heats at the thought of being caught staring at his brother.

Pierce looks nothing like his brother. Where Sean has lean muscles, Pierce is stocky. Pierce's dark brown hair has a slight wave to it, but Sean's light brown hair, whilst longer on top, makes me want to run my fingers through it.

"Just trying to get a lay of the land."

"I could always give you a better lay of the land, Pink." He gives me a wink as he leans over the reception stand. "Ever see Shoreditch in the evening?"

"Pierce, quit foolin' around and get back to work!" Sean barks from where he's bent over his table. Deep navy eyes cause fire to run through my veins. I couldn't look away from his heated gaze if I wanted to. I'm entranced.

"Looks like you've got him all riled up." He laughs to himself as he starts backing away. "If you need any assistance, Pink, just let me know."

"Much appreciated." The lie slips out easily. If I need anything, I know exactly which brother I'll be going to. And it's the one sending furious glances my way that light up my entire body. This holiday just got a whole lot more interesting.

Chapter Five

SEAN

C hrist. I made the worst snap decision of my life. Hiring the first woman who walked into the shop was a mistake. Not because Kat won't be able to do the job.

No. She's a fucking pink-haired goddess hell-bent on destroying me. With one simple touch, I've felt more for this woman than I have with all my previous girlfriends combined.

I gave her a brief tour of the shop before showing her the reservations system. Any time I caught the sweet scent of her perfume, I'd have to think of tattooing old, burly men to not get hard.

I could feel her eyes on me all morning. Any time Trevor or Pierce went to talk to her, I was breathing fire. I wanted to go over and shove them out of the way. I'm acting like a child, wanting his favourite toy back.

"Earth to Sean. What's crawled up your arse today?" Trevor kicks my boots off the table in the back room. I came back here to give myself some space. Being between appointments, I needed to breathe Kat-free air.

"Long day. Started work on that back piece and it's going to take me longer than I thought." Pierce chooses that moment to walk in.

"What are we talking about?"

"Sean has a crush."

"Called that. Anyone can see you've got the hots for Pink." I hated that stupid nickname for her. Mainly because I hated him having a connection with her. I wanted that connection with her. No way in hell am I letting them in on that secret.

"Like hell I do." It's the most bald-faced lie ever.

Trevor pierces me with a withering stare. "Bullshit. You've been shooting us death glares all day."

"Remember my no fraternization policy?"

"Okay, keep telling yourself that, bro." Trevor and Pierce share a look.

"If you two chase her off, there will be hell to pay. Now, get your arses back to work."

"Yes, sir. We don't want to mess with the boss when he so obviously does *not* have a crush on the new girl." Trevor slaps me on the back as he leaves the back room.

Fecking hell. I know these two are going to make life miserable for me.

———

"YOUR NEXT APPOINTMENT is running a few minutes late." Kat's silky voice appears over the top of the dividers between our stations.

"Appreciate it." I try not to look up at her, but damn, if I'm not drawn to her. Her long, pink hair is draped over one shoulder, and the T-shirt she's wearing hugs her curves. Curves I want to feel under my hands as I thrust into her from behind.

Shite. I need to get a handle on these thoughts, otherwise I'm going to scare her away.

"So, what all is involved in the process of tattooing someone?" Her eager blue eyes are piercing as she bites down on her bottom lip.

"You really want to know?"

She nods her head in response. "Yes. I've never gotten a tattoo before, but I've always heard so many interesting stories behind them."

I hold my arm out in front of me as I study the ink on it. From wrist to shoulder, I'm deliberate in what I put on my body. Nothing that I would want removed in a few years' time, and always something that is meaningful.

"You always have to start off with a good design."

"Like this one?" Her fingers brush over the anchor of my bicep, and it takes everything in me not to flinch away from her touch. Heat travels through me straight to my groin at the smallest touch. My eyes are drawn to her fingers moving up and down the intricate patterns, and I never want to move from this spot.

"Yes. This was one of the very first tattoos I ever gave someone. I was an apprentice at the time and fucking loved the story behind it, so it was one of my first tattoos."

"Why don't you have any on your other arm?"

I flex my right arm, slightly showing off. I'm not above trying to impress this woman. The way Pierce is hanging around and calling her Pink is driving me crazy.

"Haven't found anything I like enough to put there yet."

Her lips curve into a small smile. "So, what do you do after you have a good design?"

"Then you create a pattern and size it to how you want it on your body." I restrain myself from reaching out and touching her. "And after that, you make it permanent."

Her eyes are still focused on my arm as the chimes of the door sound, breaking her intense gaze. "Oh, sorry. Guess I better get back to it."

"If you have any more questions, just ask." Giving her a wink as she goes, I grin as her face turns the same shade as her hair. I shouldn't like how easy it is to be around her. Kat's the perfect distraction from the failure I faced with the art programme. She's only going to be here for a few weeks, and if I continue this flirting, it's going to make it even harder when she does leave.

———

Kat

AS THE LAST client leaves for the day, I lock the door behind him. Pierce and Trevor left a little while ago, and it's just me and Sean. I kept creeping over to watch him while he worked. I was fascinated by the way his arms flexed as he moved the tattoo gun easily over the skin he was working on. The designs he creates are beautiful. I can see the appeal in wanting to get a tattoo. I can only imagine having something he creates on me, his hands on my body as he works the ink into my skin.

"Are you heading home?" Sean asks, cutting off my wayward thoughts.

Right. A place to stay. I hadn't thought that far ahead. My main priority was leaving the palace without being caught, and I didn't think about where I'd be staying.

"Any chance you could direct me to a nearby hotel?"

Sean's brow furrows in confusion. "You don't have a place to stay?"

"It's okay. Just point me in the direction of where to go. I'll be fine."

He stares at me, his jaw grinding as if he's working me out. "Grab your bag and come with me." Spinning on his heel, he heads down the dark hallway towards the back of the shop. Not wanting to be left behind, I grab my bag that I stashed under the desk and hurry after him.

Next to the back door is a stairway that, it turns out, leads to a small flat. "It's not much, but you can stay here."

Trying not to make contact with Sean as he holds the door open, I take in the small space. There's a tiny kitchen to my right, a bathroom in the back, and a bed in front of the windows that can only look over the main street.

"Sean. This is too much." He's leaning against the doorframe. This entire flat could fit inside my bathroom at the palace, but I've never seen anything so wonderful.

"It's fine, Kat. Look, I don't want you wandering around the streets trying to find a place to stay." Sean is a virtual stranger, and yet I've never been shown such kindness.

I can't find the words, so standing on my tiptoes, I drop a kiss on his cheek. It's very unlike me. I'm usually much more composed as a princess, but Sean has been a true prince. My lips tingle from the contact. He hisses in response. Perhaps I'm not the only one feeling the connection between the two of us.

"Right. There are towels in the bathroom and the sheets are clean. We usually crash here after a long day, but it's been a while. You'll be safe here."

"Thank you, Sean. Truly."

He walks into the kitchen and pulls something out of the drawer. "If you need anything, here's my number." He scribbles it on a piece of paper. "And the key if you want to go out." He drops it on top of the note. He tips his head in my direction as he backs out of the room. "Have a good night, Kat."

"You too, Sean."

With the door softly closing behind him, I'm by myself for the first time. There are no advisors lurking in offices in a different part of the house. No PPOs standing guard around the building to ensure no one breaks in.

For the first time in my life, I'm well and truly alone.

Flopping onto the bed, the smile on my face is huge as it finally hits me that this is where I'll be staying the next few weeks. Instead of being on a plane to Kenya, I'm tucked away in a small room across the city. I'm doing exactly what I want to do for the first time in my life, with no one telling me I can't.

I can dance naked. I can sleep in. I can do whatever the hell I bloody please.

The buzzing in my bag pulls me out of the clouds. Seeing the familiar number, I know I have to answer.

"Hey, Jamie. What's going on?" My voice is chipper as I answer on the cheap mobile I bought at the store.

"What's going on?! Are you fucking kidding me right now? Christ, Ellie. Where the fuck are you?" Jamie's voice rings out loudly through the small studio. I have been expecting this call since I left a note for him with this number. I was rebelling, if you want to call it that, not trying to have the entire world on the lookout for me.

"Jamie, I'm fine. Really." Whenever someone asks how I am, it's always a lie. I'm fine, thanks. But for once, I am.

"You sound different. Have you been kidnapped by a cult? Alice is losing her bloody mind over here."

I can only imagine the reaction Alice had when I was supposed to be leaving for holiday and I wasn't there.

"Relax. Everything will be fine. I just needed a break."

"You were going on holiday. How is that not a break?"

Jamie's voice is confused. This is the difference between being second in line for the throne and third in line. When I have children, they will inherit the throne, so James will never have to worry about appearances like I do.

"It was not a break and you know it!" I walk over to the windows overlooking the main street. Londoners are busy going about their night. Noise drifts down the street from the corner pub. Patrons are spilling out over the sidewalk with pints in their hands. What it must be like to go to a pub every night with friends without a care in the world.

"Jamie. Please. I need this." My voice cracks with desperation. I haven't even been gone twelve hours, but I already feel calmer. Settled. Like my body is finally at ease without the weight of the entire kingdom bearing down on me.

"You're lucky I can use my royal might to keep Alice at bay, sis."

I let out a deep breath I didn't realize I was holding. "You're the best brother, you know that?"

"I'm your only brother. I'm just trying to think of how I can use this to my advantage."

There's the brother I'm used to. "I'm rolling my eyes at you."

"Oh, come off it, Ellie. I always have your back. Now are you going to tell me where you are?" I can hear the curiosity in his voice. I know it will drive him mad by not telling him.

I look around the tiny studio, a smile brightening my face. "You wouldn't believe me if I told you."

Chapter Six

KAT

"Kat!" Sean's voice booms through the small shop. It's been a busy morning, with several walk-ins coming in. It's a rush, getting to talk to all these people when they come in wanting tattoos. Not a single person has recognized me. I love the feeling of being anonymous in my own city.

Sean's told me several times to move people through, but I love talking to them. They've opened up easily about the tattoos they've wanted and the stories behind them. I love it. And the more I talk to them, the more I want my own. I keep brainstorming ideas, but I don't know if I could ever do it.

"Where are the new supplies?"

"What supplies?"

Dark pools of anger turn to look at me. "The supplies I asked you to go pick up earlier for our afternoon appointments?"

Shuffling the papers around, I see the note I wrote down this morning. "Oh, Sean. I'm so sorry. We got slammed and I completely forgot."

"How the hell am I supposed to work without the specialty colours?"

I wince as his voice increases in volume. "Can you not use the ink you have here?"

"No. It was vegan ink. I don't keep it on hand, because I never have had the request. Bloody hell, I'm going to have to cancel. I doubt they'll be a return customer."

I jump out of my seat. "No! I'll go get it now. You can delay, right?"

"No, it's going to throw off the rest of the day. I thought you said you could do this job when I hired you." Sean shakes his head and stalks off.

A lead weight settles in my stomach. I can't believe I messed up so badly. If I hadn't spent the morning talking to everyone who came into the shop, I might've remembered. I should just quit now and go back to the palace.

"You alright, darling?" A tall, leggy brunette is standing before me. She's wearing a tight dress that displays tattoos on her arms and legs.

"Sorry." I focus on the woman, trying to push my screwup out of my head. "How can I help you?"

"Is Trevor around?"

"He ran out for lunch. Did you have an appointment with him?"

"Oh well. I was going to surprise him. I finished sooner than I thought today." She extends her hand to me. "Sorry, we haven't met. I'm Ruby, Trevor's girlfriend."

"Kat. I'm the new receptionist."

"Brilliant. So not one of the ones that have hit on Trev."

"Unless you want me to hit on him, I won't be." A growl from behind me causes me to spin in my chair. Sean is glaring at the two of us before going back to what he was working on.

"Don't mind Sean," Ruby whispered. "He's been a bit of a grump lately."

I turn my attention back to her. Sean has been nothing but a gentleman to me. "I only just started, but he's been wonderful to me." A knowing smile plays on Ruby's lips.

"Sean, can I take Kat here out for lunch?"

"Fine by me. Not like I'm busy right now."

I wince at the dig.

"Fab. Grab your bag and let's go."

Ruby is out the door before I have a chance to decline. "Sean. I can go pick up everything now. I'll call them and explain it was my fault."

Deep blue eyes hit me square in the chest. I hate that I'm having such a visceral reaction to this man. Anytime I'm anywhere near him, butterflies swarm my belly.

"Sure, fine."

His brisk reaction tells me it's anything but fine. I give him a small smile before heading outside to meet Ruby. I hate that I messed this up for him. But there's the small benefit that my mistake isn't plastered all over the morning headlines for the world to see.

"Kat. It is so lovely to meet you. Tell me all about yourself." Ruby links her arm with mine. I barely hit her shoulder with the thick, platformed shoes she's wearing.

"Not much to tell. Born and raised in London and looking for a change in my life, so figured why not start at a tattoo shop."

"And what do you think of our Sean?" I smile at the way she says *our Sean*.

"Not sure what you want to know. I've only known him a few days, but he's been quite nice to me. Especially for giving me the job." Even though I'm not very good at said job.

Ruby stops at a kebab cart on the corner of the street.

"The best kebabs in London," she states, ordering us each one. After we each get our lunch, I walk us in the direction of the tube. Even if I messed up Sean's appointment, I still want to get the supplies to show him I take this job seriously.

"Are you attracted to Sean?" Ruby breaks the silence as I bite into my kebab to delay my answer. Holy shite, this really is the best. Am I attracted to Sean? How could I not be? The instant spark when I met him was undeniable. But I have to fight this attraction. There is no possible way I can get involved with someone. I'm a princess. No matter what I'm leading myself to believe right now, the real world will come back up to meet me in no time.

"It doesn't matter," I say.

"Brilliant. That's all I need to know." That sly grin is back on her face.

"Why's that all you need to know?"

"Ruby! Kat! What are you doing over here?" Trevor jogs up to us from the opposite direction.

"I finished up early, so wanted to surprise you with lunch. But I met Kat here instead."

"And what do you think?" They exchange a glance that only years of trust and intimacy can establish.

"I think we should invite Kat to Sunday lunch."

"Hell, yes!" Trevor's voice echoes through the street.

"What about Sunday lunch?" My gaze darts between the two of them.

"You'll just have to come and find out."

———

THE REST of the week went by without issue, but I was treading lightly around Sean. There's nothing worse than getting on someone's bad side, and I didn't want to disappoint him. I wanted to prove to myself that I could do this. That I was more than just a pampered princess.

Trevor and Ruby host everyone for Sunday lunch since the shop is closed. Sundays are usually a light day for me, meaning only two events, followed by an evening off. We used to have family meals together growing up, but with our own royal duties, we stopped them altogether.

I find the small building where they live, and Ruby is opening the door before I have a chance to knock. Her outfit shines brighter than her personality. A cheetah print crop top accents her lime-green mini skirt. She's the most colourful person I've ever met. I look tame in my jeans and jumper by comparison.

"Kat, darling! I'm so happy you could make it." She pulls me in for a hug like we're old friends. We've chatted a few times this week, but it's hard not to be sucked into Ruby's bubble. "Come in, come in."

She sweeps me into their house. Bright purple paint is splashed across the walls. A set of stairs leads up to a bedroom that overlooks the living room. The kitchen in the back opens up to a backyard, a rarity in London. The laughter of three men filters in through the open door.

"This place is brilliant, Ruby."

"Perfect spot in Shoreditch. It's all we need."

Pierce comes through the door and sweeps me in for a hug. Pierce reminds me so much of Jamie. While Sean has an invisible weight holding him down, Pierce doesn't seem to have a care in the world. Maybe it's why I'm so drawn to Sean. I know what it's like to have the weight of expectations bearing down on you.

"Pink! I didn't think you would come. Want anything to drink?"

"A proper Sunday roast? I wouldn't turn that down for anything," I laugh.

"And here I thought I was finally getting a girlfriend." Ruby shakes her head in my direction as she hands me a cocktail. "Cheers to new friends." She gives me a wink as we all toast. "Now, Pierce. Head back outside with the men so we women can finish up in here."

I give her a look, but she shakes her head. Pierce just shrugs and walks back outside. Sean's laugh hits me and I feel it everywhere. Damn it, Ellie. You're not supposed to be feeling like this.

Trying to distract myself, I ask Ruby what I can help with.

"Oh, I didn't need help. Trevor does all of the cooking. I set the table, and that's already done. I just want to chat without the ears of those nosey Nellies outside listening in."

I snort over the drink in my hand. "You are quite the deceptive one, Ruby."

"And yet, none of the boys have figured it out." She shakes her head as she leads me over to their grey velvet couch. "How has your first week gone? Aside from the small mishap?"

My face still burns hot at the thought of messing up. It's been ingrained in me since I was a child that I should be someone the people can lean on. So whenever I make a mistake, it's hard to push past it.

"Uneventful. Which is what anyone would want, I guess."

"And Sean? Treating you well?" Her eyes glimmer with mischief.

"What's this all about?" I return her look with equal measure.

"I'm just calling it like I see it. There's something between you two." I smile into my drink as I take a large gulp.

48

"How can you tell? We've hardly been around you."

"You have so much to learn. Those three men out there are the biggest gossips in London. Trevor came home last week raving about you. Said he's never seen Sean look at someone like he looks at you."

"That can't possibly be true."

She shakes her head at me. "And yet it is." The timer on the oven dings, and chaos descends upon the kitchen. Everyone comes inside, and plates are passed around as the roast, potatoes, pudding, and stuffing are all divvied up.

"We're eating outside, so go ahead." Ruby ushers us all outside as the delicious smells waft over me. Being the last out, the only remaining seat is next to Sean. Ruby and Trevor are grinning like fools at me. All part of their master plan.

Strands of colourful lights are hung across the top of their small garden, while a fountain trickles in the corner. It's the perfect oasis in the heart of London.

"Ever had a Sunday roast like this?" Sean's voice is quiet as he leans into me.

Sunday lunch at the palace usually consisted of four different types of meat, any type of pudding you could imagine, and every kind of potato you could make. But this? This is simple. And decadent. And bloody perfect.

"This would be a first." I cut off a large piece of meat and shovel it into my mouth. "Trevor, this is fecking incredible." I take another very unprincess-like bite. Sean laughs next to me as I savour the meal in front of me.

"You're welcome round any time, Kat." Trevor's leaning back, his arm thrown around Ruby.

"And I gladly accept." Shite, I don't know why I said that. It's not a promise I can keep. I so desperately want to keep it, but my time here is fleeting.

"Sean also makes a crack roast if you want to try his."

Ruby waggles her eyebrows in my direction. These two could not be more transparent. They are playing the role of matchmaker today. And if I wasn't a temporary person in their life, I would willingly give in.

"A man who can cook? I like the sound of that." I lean back in my chair, my arm resting against Sean's. I make no move to pull away. Heat radiates from the contact through my body.

"Breakfast is my specialty. I make a mean bangers and mash." Sean's deep blue eyes lock onto mine and don't move. Lust takes over my body, as need coils deep in my core. I'd love to have this man make me breakfast.

"I can't say anyone has ever made me bangers before." I swipe another bite of pudding, letting the fork linger on my lips. The blue of Sean's eyes disappears as they widen, focused solely on my mouth.

"I'll be sure to make it for you then, love." A swarm of butterflies takes up residence in my stomach when Sean's hand moves down to my thigh and gives it a squeeze. It's the smallest of touches, but I'm completely bewildered by this man. He leaves his hand where it is as he goes back to eating lunch.

My body is swirling with emotion and arousal. It's a bad idea to let these emotions run wild in me, but there's this connection with Sean. Every day I'm around him, it grows stronger. I'm distracted and unfocused when he's near.

"We're going to go inside and get dessert. C'mon, Pierce." Ruby taps him on the shoulder to follow them in.

"Why can't I stay out here?" Ruby rolls her eyes at him as Trevor whispers in his ear. A huge grin spreads across his face.

"We'll be back." He winks at us, before following the other two inside.

"I doubt we'll be seeing those three anytime soon." Sean leans back in his chair, pushing his plate in front of him.

"They aren't exactly subtle." I take a sip of my drink, trying to look anywhere but at Sean.

"Kat." His voice is smooth like whisky. Goose pimples break out over my skin. My eyes are magnets to his. "You catch on quickly. No one has ever accused those three of being subtle."

"That's a nice way of saying they're a bunch of wankers. Who raised you to be such a proper gentleman?" My voice comes out on a laugh to break the tension.

"That would be my mum." He sips on his gin and tonic, the liquid sitting on his lips as his tongue darts out to lick it off. What I wouldn't give to be able to lean over and lick it off myself.

Shaking myself out of my thoughts, I go back to the conversation at hand. "Does your mum live in London?"

"They live outside of the city. Dad is a professor and travels a good portion of the year now, so Mum goes with him. They like being by themselves now. We see them enough, so can't complain. How 'bout you?"

His question catches me off guard. It seems no matter what I say, I would give them away. But it's my own insecurities. Sean has no idea who I am. There's no spark of recognition on his face.

"We see each other regularly. Sometimes more than I'd like."

He just gives me that playful smirk of his. "One of the perks of your parents not living close. You can still be close, without being physically close. Don't get me wrong, I love them. But sometimes Mum can be a little overbearing."

"As any good mum should be."

"I can only imagine your mum. Chasing after a little pink-haired toddler."

I throw my head back in laughter. "Do you really think I had pink hair as a little girl?"

"Fine. Purple?" His smile is playful, but no less sultry, as he pins me with a heated stare.

The spring day has nothing on the heat surrounding us. Sean's hand is still on my leg, drawing lazy circles. Each swipe of his thumb sends another jolt of desire through me. I could combust I'm so worked up. My mind is blank as I try to think of anything to break the heated moment between the two of us. I want this moment with Sean more than I've wanted anything in my life.

But our connected fates are temporary. It's written in the sand. Fleeting at best. Whatever this is, it won't last.

"You alright, love?" There's that nickname again. Sean's warm, calloused hand covers mine, and I instinctively turn my hand to hold his.

I give him my best princess smile. "I couldn't be better."

Chapter Seven

SEAN

I can't figure out Kat to save my life. And it's driving me up the bloody wall. That smile she gave me at Trevor's was fake. She's so tight-lipped on where she's from that I can't get a read on her. But everyone that comes into the shop immediately falls for her. She's a ray of fucking sunshine welcoming everyone into the shop. You can't help but be pulled under her spell.

Shaking off my wayward thoughts of Kat, I clean up my station for the night. It was an easy day. Steady, but not overly busy with walk-ins.

"So, how has everything been going?" Kat hasn't made a mistake since her first week here. I could see how much she hated doing it, and it made me feel like a wanker for making her feel bad about it.

"It's been great. I never thought I'd get to meet so many wonderful people."

I shake my head at her comment. "You watch too much TV. Not everyone who gets a tattoo is in a motor-cycle club or gang."

A blush spreads across her pale skin, and it makes her even sexier. "That's not what I thought. I guess I thought they would be more gruff and surly. Not in biker gangs."

"Well, I'm glad they proved you wrong."

Kat's gaze lingers on me, as if she's studying me, trying to uncover something about me. "Want to have dinner with me? My treat for messing up last week."

"Kat. You don't need to buy me dinner. It was an honest mistake."

She's chewing on her bottom lip. I want to pull it out and suck on it myself.

"Fine. As a thank you for the job then."

She is not going to take no for an answer.

"Why are you so hell-bent on going to the pub tonight? It's just bad pub food and drunk arseholes watching the match." I give her a weary side-eye.

"Because I haven't had fish and chips in ages. I want greasy pub food and a pint." She clasps her hands under her chin, batting those big, blue eyes at me. I don't know what this thing going on between us is, but every time I'm around her, I want to stay in her world. Her sexy smile and unassuming laugh suck me in.

"Bloody hell. Let's go. But I'm buying." I point a finger at her as I go to close up the shop.

"As long as you're coming, I won't complain." She claps her hands in front of her as she turns off the harsh overhead lights. The old bulbs cast her in a heavenly glow. The way her hair is pulled up makes her look like an angel with a pink halo.

Fuck, if I don't get these feelings for her under control, I'm going to be sporting a semi all the way to dinner. And I don't want to scare her off.

"Ready?" she asks, a soft smile playing on her lips.

"Let's go." Kat walks down the back hall, and my eyes are drawn to the sway of her arse. Christ, it's a good one. And it's doing nothing to alleviate the pressure in my groin. There's going to be a permanent indent from my zipper on my dick if I'm not careful.

It's a cool spring night when we step out onto the main road. Being a weeknight, there aren't as many people out and about.

"I love London on nights like this." Kat's voice is quiet as she looks around the street. It's not busy. "It's almost quiet. Makes you feel like you're in a small town and not one of the world's biggest cities."

I study her as she speaks. There's that inkling again. The one I can't describe because she's keeping part of herself closed off from me. "I think you might be the only person that feels that way."

"So be it. Now, where's the best pub for fish and chips around here?"

"The Owl and Pussycat."

"Are you serious?" Kat asks on a laugh.

"Best pub around. You'll get your fish and chips, but they also have billiards if you care to try your hand."

"Well then, lead the way."

We make the short walk together, the setting sun lighting the sky on fire. Noise drifts out from the pub as lads are standing outside smoking with pints in their hands. We nudge past them into the crowded pub and thankfully find an empty booth in the corner. The table is still sticky from whoever was here last.

"What'll it be?" The waitress is abrupt as she appears at the end of the table.

"Two lagers and two fish and chips." She doesn't give us a second glance before she leaves the table. Not two minutes later, two pints are dropped off as she rushes off to the next table.

Kat's eyes are roving all around the pub. I've never seen someone so excited to be eating cheap food in a grubby bar.

"So is this living up to your pub dreams?" I clink my glass against hers. I watch her throat work as she takes a long drink. Fecking hell. I don't know how I got in so deep. Everything about her is mesmerizing, from the slope of her neck to the soft curve of her lips as she stares up at me. Her eyes give her away. Whether she's happy or upset, I know just by looking into her eyes.

"This is brilliant. Cheers." She taps her glass against mine again and finishes off half her beer in one swallow.

"Easy there, love. We've got all night."

"Sorry. Just happy to be out tonight."

"You haven't been staying at the flat every night, have you?"

She takes another longer gulp of her beer, as her cheeks flush. "And what if I have been?"

Foam lingers on her upper lip, and it takes everything I have not to lean over and lick it off.

"I figured you'd be out with Ruby every night. She really likes you."

"Ruby is wonderful. But I don't think she wants to be pulled away from Trevor."

I tap my finger to my temple. "Those two are connected at the hip. Bit disgusting, really."

Two baskets of fish and chips are set down in front of us. "Need anything else?"

"Few more beers, please," Kat responds before I can get a word in. She finishes off her drink before diving into the greasiest basket of food. I watch as it happens—Kat tears off a steaming bite, and regret is written across her face.

"Hot! Hot! Hot!" She reaches across the table and takes a swig of my beer.

"You alright there, love?" Covering her mouth with her hand, she gives me a shy look.

"Sorry. Just couldn't help myself. Even hot, that is delicious."

"Did you doubt me and think I would take you anywhere where they served crap?" I tuck into my own dinner with more care than Kat.

"I should know better." She winks at me. A wink I feel everywhere. Damn it. What the bloody hell is going on with me? I've never been so taken with a woman before. Kat's only temporary. She even told me as much when I gave her the position. I should be focusing on the shop and not getting distracted by Kat. But here I am, falling for her.

———

"YOU'RE QUITE PRETTY, you know that?" The hiccup tells me Kat has had one too many pints.

We didn't make it to billiards. Kat was sucking back beer like it was going to dry up tomorrow. As she takes another sip of her beer, I grab the glass from her hands.

"I think that's enough for you."

"Let's go take a boat ride!"

"I'm sorry, a boat ride?" I can't imagine what's gotten into her pretty little head.

"Yes. I've always wanted to sail around the Thames. It'd be a fab idea today." Her lazy eyes lock in on mine.

"Not tonight, Kat."

"You're no fun, Sean." She pouts those pretty lips at me.

"Sorry, love. But you'll thank me tomorrow when you don't feel like a train wreck." Calling the waitress over, I pay for our meal and pull Kat out of the booth. The sway of her body into mine is a dead giveaway on how many pints she had.

"Can I thank you with a kiss?"

This woman is going to be the death of me.

"You're drunk, Kat." Her arms wrap around my waist as I lead us through the crowd and out into the now cold night. She shivers against me. I pull her closer to me, trying to keep her warm. I love the feel of her tucked against me. No matter how much I keep trying to tell myself I shouldn't want her, she sucks me in.

"But you want to kiss me?" *More than I want my next breath.*

"I'm not going to kiss you tonight."

"Why don't you want to kiss me?" She stops and leans against the building, giving me her best pout.

"I'm not going to kiss you when you're bloody well pissed."

She turns her hazy, drunk eyes on me. "But you do want to kiss me?"

I lean into her, letting her feel my very obvious desire for her. Kat runs her hands through the scruff on my jaw, lighting up every cell in my body. Christ, this woman is going to kill me.

"Yes, Kat. But the first time I kiss you isn't going to be when you're drunk."

She's biting her bottom lip as she focuses in on me. I lean closer, cupping her face in my hands. It would be so easy to take what I want. "Because, Kat,"—I pull her lip out of the clutches of her teeth and a quiet gasp escapes her lips—"because when I kiss you, I want you to remember it. Because when I do kiss you, it will be the only kiss you'll ever want to remember. It will be the best kiss of your life."

"Cocky much?"

"Confident, not cocky."

Chapter Eight

KAT

U gh. Between the pounding in my head and the sun streaming into the windows, I want to die.

Die of a wicked hangover and of embarrassment. I drank enough last night to feel terrible, but not enough to forget what I did. Or I should say, what I didn't do.

Why did I ask to kiss him? Pulling the pillow over my head, I curl back under the covers. It's safe under here. I don't have to go downstairs and face Sean if I stay here all day.

No such luck. The pounding in my head echoes on the door into the flat. "Go away."

"Kat. Open the door!" Ruby's voice carries through the small space. At least facing Ruby is less embarrassing than facing Sean.

Climbing out of bed, I notice I'm not in my own clothes. Not sure where I got them from, I open the door for Ruby and head right back over to bed.

"Looks like someone had a good night." She jumps onto the bed next to me, jostling my sensitive head.

"I wouldn't call it a good night."

Ruby looks around. "Well, no. Unless Sean ditched you this morning."

I sit up too fast and clutch my head. "He was the perfect gentleman. I threw myself at him like a cat in heat."

"Well, I do come bearing gifts." She hands over a cup of tea and pulls out pastries from the bag sitting between us.

"You are a queen." I want to take the words back as soon as I say them. I've been so careful, but I don't want anyone to guess who I am. No one would give a second glance to the girl with pink hair, but if you stopped and stared, one could put two and two together. "Wait, how'd you know I drank too much last night?"

"Sean may have called me to pop over on my way to school this morning."

"Why does he have to be so perfect?" I moan, breaking the croissant apart and shoving it in my mouth.

Ruby shakes her head at me. "Oh, he's so not perfect. He wouldn't do this for anyone else. Just you."

"Ruby! That makes it even worse. I can't face him today!" I shove my face into my hands, wearing embarrassment like a second skin.

"You can and you will. I only have so much time before school, and I'll go downstairs with you. It won't be weird unless you make it weird."

I give her the side-eye. "It's going to be weird. I called Sean pretty and pouted like a toddler when I didn't get my way."

"I'm sure he's seen worse with Pierce's women."

"And I'm not one of those women. I've never gotten so pissed in my life, and the first time was in front of Sean!" I throw myself back on the bed in a rather dramatic fashion. Being second in line to the throne, I'm always careful about how much I drink when I'm out. I never want to be overserved and cause the paparazzi to question if I have a drinking problem.

"I guess that means we need to have girls' night so you won't be so drunk next time." She says this like it's no big deal. But inside, my roiling stomach stills.

It's always been hard to make friends. Everyone always had an ulterior motive so I was wary. The few who stuck around long enough were like shooting stars. Bright for that time in my life, but then faded to the background because they hated the press.

But after meeting Ruby, I don't want to lose her. I have no idea what will happen, but she is one of the most genuine people I've met. She hides her tattoos when she goes to work, but her colourful personality still shines through with her bright wardrobe.

Whether it's the lingering effects of the alcohol from last night or this woman taking me under her wing, I pull her to me in a crushing hug.

"What's this all about?" She doesn't hesitate, wrapping her arms around me.

"It's always been hard for me to make girlfriends. So it's nice to actually have one."

"Kat, you are stuck with me. I am surrounded by too much male energy. Don't get me wrong, I love those boys, but a little feminine energy around would go a long way to bringing them down a peg or two."

I give her an extra squeeze before letting her go. "I guess I should get cleaned up and face the music."

"That's the spirit, love. Besides, if Sean didn't kick you out of here last night, I'm betting that's a good sign."

———

THE SHOP IS ALREADY BUSTLING with excitement when I get downstairs.

"It's still early. Why are there people here?"

"Oh, shite. You don't know. It's their flash day. Once every few months, they'll do set designs for people for a flat fee. In and out. Cheap and easy. All the guys do it for the day. Busy, but it's fun."

"Why didn't you start with that?" I slap her on the arm, heading over to the desk where there's a line of people.

"You wouldn't let me get a word in edgewise, love." She gives me a wink as she heads over to Trevor before leaving.

Summoning what courage I have, I walk over to where Sean is inking a tattoo onto someone's arm. It's beautiful, like everything he does.

"Morning, Kat. How you feeling?" Sean's smile only increases the tension in my body. It's coiling so tight that I could snap like a rubber band.

"Good. How can I help?"

"Just start taking names as they come in. We get to them in the order they arrive as soon as we're done."

"How long does this go on?" There's a line out the door.

"We take people until three, but we stay until everyone is done. So buckle up, love."

There isn't time to be embarrassed about how I acted last night. Sean is too busy tattooing as many people as are coming in the door.

"Hi there, ladies. Names and designs, please."

"Doll, that is some fab pink hair! How did you get it done?"

I pat my hair down, self-conscious of these two women

staring at me. I can't tell them I started out with brown hair and bleached it before adding the color, or they may figure out who I am. "I just got a box from the store. You really like it?"

"It's brilliant! You think I could pull this off?" She turns to her friend. "I don't care. I want to try it anyway. You look fab."

"Thank you." My smile is shy, as I've never had someone praise my appearance. It's a contrast to what I'm used to hearing. My wayward thoughts stray to the man who is now standing behind me. It's crazy after such a short time that I can feel his presence behind me without having to look.

"Pink looks good on her." Heat radiates from his palm at my waist. "Sorry, need this for the next appointment." He's looking over my shoulder at the waiting list. I can't focus on anything but his overwhelming presence. The clean scent that is all Sean threatens to overtake me. "Ladies, we'll be with you soon."

Sean gives me a gentle squeeze before going back to work. I sway into the warmth he left behind. I crave this man with a desire I've never felt. The closeness I felt to him last night was something I want to experience now. Without the blur of alcohol.

"Bloody hell, he is sex on a stick." My gaze swings from Sean's retreating form to the two women in front of me. "Are you screwing him?"

My mouth opens and closes. She grins and continues, "Sorry, that was rude. Sometimes I have no filter. But you're one lucky woman."

"Thanks. We'll be with you soon." There's not much I can say after that. I make my way through the line, my thoughts and gaze drifting to Sean as the guys work through the long list of customers. I've never seen such an operation before. I'm in awe of how the guys are working through the crowds today.

The shop has never been busier, and I love it. Finally having a moment to breathe as the line dwindles down, I catch bits and pieces of the conversations happening in line.

"Did you see the latest royal scandal?" My ears perk up at that. Latest royal scandal? What in the bloody hell is going on now?

Looking around, I ensure that no one is paying any attention to me. There's too much going on today. Sneaking away to a quiet spot, I pull up the news and I start fuming. I wouldn't be surprised if steam was coming out of my ears.

Prince James caught in a scandalous position with mystery woman. Might our playboy prince have finally found his princess?

A RED HEAD, not his usual type, is glued to Jamie, with her hand down his pants. If I were caught in this position, I would be set on fire by the press. But Jamie? It's only the prince looking for his princess. I keep scrolling, the headlines causing an anger I've never felt before to take over.

A night with Princess Eleanor! Get an exclusive with a man who has shared the Princess's bed. Is she really ready to lead our nation?

YOU HAVE GOT to be fucking kidding me. Jamie finds his princess, and they are questioning if I am ready to lead the nation? I've only been learning to be queen my entire life.

"You hiding from me?" I jump out of my skin at Sean's sneaky presence behind me. Rage is making my brain fuzzy.

"Why would you say that?" I slide my phone in my back pocket, not wanting him to see what I was looking at.

"You've been twitchy all day. Are you stressing about last night?" Sean rests his hand just above my head, leaning over. He's all-consuming. I can barely think straight.

"I was earlier," I whisper, "but not anymore." No. Now, my embarrassment has been quickly replaced with anger. Anger at the press. Anger at my brother. Anger at being told to be the perfect princess at all times, yet still no one believes I can be queen.

"I want a tattoo," I blurt out. Sean pulls back, his face staying even.

"And what's bringing this on?" His hand drops lower, hovering by my face.

"Because I want one! Because we work in a tattoo parlour. Because I trust you." I shove Sean out of the way, pacing the small space at the back of the shop.

My skin is tight as I'm buzzing with energy. It's the final straw. Every single thing I've done in my life is in service to others. For the first time in my life, I'm living for me. And getting this reminder, while I'm here, is a slap in the face. To the press. To the crown. To my entire life that I am no longer happy with. To the fact that no matter what I do, I will never be held to an equal standard as my brother.

"Kat. You need to breathe." Sean stills me, his arms on my biceps. "You don't need to get a tattoo."

"But I want one!" I shout.

"I'll give her a tattoo if you won't." Pierce squeezes past Sean as he grabs more supplies.

Fire lights Sean's eyes. "Piss off, Pierce."

He smirks at Sean as he leaves us be. It helps to dissipate some of my anger.

"Do you even have a design in mind?"

"Wildflowers." It's the first thing that comes to mind, but I know it's right.

"And where would you put it?"

"What's with the twenty questions?" I flex my hands at my sides, trying to push past the surge of anger coursing through me.

His fingers brush a stray lock of hair behind my ear. It's a caring touch, one I lean into. "I don't want you to make a decision you regret. You can't just wipe it off."

"I won't regret it, Sean." I'm toying with the hem of his shirt, not able to look him in the eye. "It's you or no one else."

"Has anyone ever told you no before?"

The laughter in his voice pushes out the final flares of anger that have a hold over me.

"You'd be surprised." I pierce him with a stare he won't be able to refuse.

"I'm going to do this, aren't I?"

Yes, yes, he is.

Chapter Nine

SEAN

"Are you absolutely sure? These are permanent." I give her another stare. She's only been here a short time, and she made a snap decision. Being in the business, you get a sense of when people will regret their decisions. I'm not getting that from Kat, but I have to be sure.

"Positive." The gleam in her eye tells me not to ask again. Message received.

"Alright. Let me get it on transfer paper and we can get started." The design turned out even better than I imagined. Sometimes, it's so hard bringing a client's vision to life. Sometimes, things don't turn out exactly how they want. But when it does? I fucking love it when they see it and are blown away.

Kat's reaction when she saw her design? The smile lit up her entire face. It was practically glowing when she saw her idea come to life. It's why I love doing what I do.

It's eerily quiet in here tonight. We're doing it after hours. Coming back around to my station, the overhead lights are dim, lighting Kat up like an angel. She has the look. The look all people have before they get their first tattoo. The excitement and nerves battling it out in her eyes.

"Don't worry, love. It'll be great." She's chewing on that bottom lip. The one I've wanted to suck between my lips since she told me she wanted to kiss me the other night at the pub. Damn her and those kissable lips.

"I wouldn't want anyone else's hands on me for this." That simmering look in her eyes causes a stirring deep in my chest. I don't know what it is about Kat, but every time I'm near her, I have the same visceral reaction. Heat like nothing I've ever felt before courses through my veins whenever she is near. I know she feels the same way. Her throat clearing breaks me out of my thoughts.

"Right. You're going to need to lose the shirt, and I'll get this put on and you tell me what you think. Placement, size. If you want to change it, speak now or forever hold your peace."

"Clever. How often do you say that?" Her eyes are bright as she pulls the T-shirt over her head. I look away, even though I know my hands will be on her for the next few hours.

"Only to the pretty girls." She shakes her head at me as she drops her shirt on the chair next to my stand. "Now, come stand over here so I can get this on you."

The sweet floral scent of her perfume wafts over me as she stands between my legs. The gentle curve of her waist is soft beneath my fingers as I go about applying the stencil. Once I'm happy with where it is, I smooth it over her pale skin, peeling it back. It took me a few days to get the design just right, but Kat's reaction is why I love what I do.

She had tears in her eyes when she first saw it. Blues, pinks, and purples mixed together, creating a wildness that's hard to capture. It matches the woman I'm tattooing. This bright, whirlwind of a woman.

"Alright, go see how it looks." Walking over to the full-length mirror, she lifts her arm to see the final product. Her breath catches in her throat.

"Sean. It's amazing. Truly." Her delicate fingers trace the pattern over and over. The vines, the flowers, the leaves, everything. "It's better than I ever could have dreamed of." The awe in her voice has me wanting to puff out my chest and sing my own praises. But I don't. Instead, I call her back over to the chair and help her lie down at the right angle.

"Okay, just relax for a few minutes while I get every-thing sorted, then we'll get started."

She looks at me, a knowing look in her eyes. "You're really good at this."

"What?" I look up at her from where I'm getting my station ready. I love this part—making sure everything is perfect before I get started. The colours, the right needles. It's always been calming to me, especially with the chaos of the last few months of my programme tanking.

"Putting people at ease. I always thought tattoo artists were these big gruff people without a lot of feelings."

"Tell me how you really feel."

"Oh, shut it. I'm serious. It takes a certain kind of person to make people feel okay when getting a tattoo. I notice it every time someone comes in."

There's a twinge in my chest, and I like it. I like that she pays attention to how I treat my clients. I have worked hard to get where I am today. I try to play off how much it affects me that she notices. "Well, I don't want people crying and screaming in the shop. People might think it's a torture chamber."

The small laugh that escapes her further lights me up. Damn it, why is she affecting me so much?

Having set the last of my tools up, I buzz the gun a few times to find the right setting. "Ready?"

"As I'll ever be." She swings her arm over her head as I dip the gun into the coloured ink.

"If you want me to stop at any time, just say so. As long as you're comfortable, we can go as long as you like."

"I'm sure you'd like to prove how long you can go." Her smirk tells me she didn't miss the innuendo behind my comment.

Setting my hand on her side, I apply a decent amount of pressure to hold her down. The first pass of the gun can be jarring for some. I notice the small goose pimples that break out over her skin at my touch. I shouldn't like it as much as I do, but damn, do I ever.

Stepping on the pedal, I make my first pass as I start tracing the stalks of the flowers.

"Shite, is it going to hurt that much?" She tries to peek over her shoulder at me, but she's at too awkward of an angle on the table.

"Sorry, love, but probably more. It's not bad starting out but hurts more as we go."

"Damn. Alright, keep going." She squeezes her eyes closed as I start again. The sound of the gun is hypnotic. Every time I do this, I get lost in my thoughts. It makes it easier for me to forget it's Kat on the table. That my hands are gingerly moving up and down her side as I permanently alter her body. I can't wait to see the finished product on her side.

"So why is this one special, Kat?"

"What?" Her voice is pained as it squeaks out.

"Do you need a break?" I haven't done much, but for newbies, it can hurt.

"No. No, I'm okay. It feels like my skin is on fire, but

shite, no stopping." Her skin is turning a fiery red, but I won't tell her that.

"Okay, concentrate on me then. Tell me why this tattoo is special."

She blows out a breath, trying to calm her nerves as I keep moving the gun over her skin, wiping excess ink off as I go.

"It reminds me of my grandfather. He's a very important person in my life."

"How so?" The more I can keep her talking, the less she'll want to focus on the pain.

"He was always around when I was growing up. He has a house in Scotland where we would spend summer holidays, and I loved the wildflowers there. He'd take me on long walks after supper. Just me and him. It was our special time together. He calls me Wildflower."

"He sounds like a nice guy." It reminds me of my own granddad, even though I don't get to see him all that often.

"Everyone loves him. It will be quite hard to live up to his memory," she whispers, almost as if I'm not meant to hear.

I pull the gun back and stare at her face, scrunched up, as if this memory is causing her pain. "Why would you need to live up to his memory?"

"Don't you want to live up to your granddad's legacy? Or even your dad's?"

"My dad is a university professor. Quite renowned, if you will, in the world of physics," I laugh. I would never be able to live up to his reputation.

"How did he take you wanting to be a tattoo artist then? Did he want you to follow in his footsteps?"

"Christ, no. I would've been a terrible professor. I hated school growing up. I did enough to get by but went to school for art instead." I dip the gun into the green ink again and continue making progress on the base of the flowers.

"But he wasn't upset with you that you didn't like academia growing up?"

"Mum supported us in everything we do, still does, and he is crazy about her, so it wouldn't have mattered."

"Must be nice." Her voice is wistful. It's driving me mad that I can't figure Kat out. She's so quiet about her past and where she came from that I have no idea what to make of it.

"Do you not get a lot of choices?"

"My future was determined from the day I was born. It must be nice to have such a supportive mum."

"She's the best. She's American, you know."

"How ghastly!" She laughs. "How'd she end up across the pond?"

"Uni. She loved England so much she convinced my granddad to send her to school here. I think he was hoping it would cure her of her love of everything British. A week into school, she met my dad, and they've been together ever since."

"That's so sweet. You said they don't live in London, right?"

My plan of distracting her is working. The muscles under my hands feel more relaxed than they did when I started. It's always easier to tattoo someone who isn't tense with pain.

"They live out in the country now. My dad took a job at a smaller university but travels more and does speeches across the continent. Mum goes with him. They are blissfully happy."

"I wish I could be blissfully happy like that." She sighs, her curves moving under my hands. I linger longer than necessary when wiping the ink off, savouring how she feels under my fingers. Wondering what it would feel like to be on top of her. Shite, I shouldn't be having these thoughts right now. I need to be professional.

"And why aren't you blissfully happy, Kat?"

"I'm not exactly doing what I really want to in life."

"And why can't you make a change?"

I rest the gun on the table as she turns to face me.

"It's not that simple for me. I can't change what I want to do like some people."

"Could you learn to be happy? I mean, are you happy right now?" I hate the feeling that Kat isn't happy. It's rare when Kat doesn't have a smile on her face. She's never seemed unhappy here.

"I'm the happiest I've been in a long time, Sean."

I can't hide the grin that comes over me when she says this. "Well hopefully, wherever you land, you'll continue to be happy."

She's quiet now as I finish the last of the stems. This part is easy. The shading is going to take some time to go back and fill in after.

"Why don't you take a break, and I'll get the next batch of colours ready to go?"

"Can I take a peek?" she asks.

"If you want. It's going to be all red right now. I promise, the flowers won't look bloody when it's done."

She laughs at me as she walks over to the mirror, wincing only slightly. Her eyes widen as she sees the progress I've made.

"We're only a quarter of the way there?" Her voice is a little high.

"More or less. I still have shading to do once I fill in the colours."

Her face pales as she looks back at the mirror, taking in the work I've done.

"We don't have to finish in one session. Lots of people come back to finish."

"No!" she shouts, turning to face me. "I mean, no. It needs to be done tonight. I'll be okay. Just give me a few minutes to rest."

"Take all the time you need, love." I pat her knee as she sits down on the table. Her hair is a tangled mess from lying on it. She couldn't look sexier if she tried.

"Do you ever get tired while doing this?"

"I've got good stamina," I say, winking as I finish pouring the colours into the tiny caps on my tray.

"I'll be sure to leave that in my review then."

She lies back on the table, getting situated again. "Alright, let's get this over with."

"Just what every man wants to hear."

———

"YOU READY TO LOOK NOW?" I wipe the rest of the ink off and put more cream on her skin. Angry red blotches and dots of blood mar her now tattooed side.

"I've only been waiting for hours."

"It's been three hours. Some people have pieces that take over ten."

She sways slightly as she sits up. "You alright, love?" I ask.

Kat nods slowly, tilting her face up to look at me. "Just a little woozy, that's all."

"Let me give you a hand." Grabbing her elbow, I help her off the table and steer her towards the mirror to show her the finished product.

She's quiet. Her eyes move over the pattern as she takes it all in. "Sean. I..." she starts but can't finish. When her eyes meet mine in the mirror, they're glassy. Shit, does she not like it?

Before I know what's happening, her arms are around my neck and her lips are crashing against mine. It takes me point-two seconds to get my wits about me. Mindful of the likely screaming pain her side is in, I settle one hand low on her hip and slip the other into her hair, easily taking control. Christ, I've wanted to kiss this woman since she walked into my shop.

I slide my tongue along the seam of her lips, and she easily grants me entrance. Kat tastes like the cup of tea she had before we started, and it's intoxicating. The velvet of her tongue tangles with mine as she meets me stroke for stroke. The soft gasp that escapes tells me she can feel how hard I am for her. Tipping her head to the side, I trail kisses down her jaw to her ear.

The moan that escapes her has me shifting and pressing her against the mirror as I nibble down her neck. Shite, her skin is perfect. I want to bite and mark her as mine so no man will ever look at her.

Trying to be aware of her aching skin, I pull back ever so slightly, pressing my forehead to hers. Her eyes are half-closed, lips swollen from our heady kiss.

"So, I take it you like your tattoo then?" A smirk plays on my lips. Looking up at me, she stares into my eyes, a few pink hairs ghosting across her face.

"Sean, it is the most beautiful thing I've ever seen in my life. I can't believe it's on me. Forever now. A piece of you will always be with me."

Christ, now I'm ready to tattoo these bloody flowers on my skin so I can carry her with me. How the hell did I get in so deep with this woman, and what in the fecking hell am I going to do about it?

Chapter Ten

The pinch in my side pulls me awake. Getting out of the small bed, I head into the bathroom to look at the new tattoo on my side. The skin is an angry red. But underneath it is the most beautiful and intricate pattern. I can see why people love getting them. The flowers are a perfect match to the ones at the castle we would visit in the summer. It brings a smile to my face to have them here.

I loved those summers more than anything. There was no pressure to be the perfect princess or to look and act a certain way. Behind those castle walls, it was just family. Those days spent with Granddad there were some of my favourites. They were few and far between. And now, as a delayed act of teenage rebellion, I'll carry those memories with me in a more permanent way.

I trace the still tender skin, where Sean's hands inked me. My body was buzzing with need the entire time. I can still feel the pressure of his hand on my hip as the needle moved over my skin. I couldn't help my reaction. His lips were so soft and firm, I can't help but want more of them. I want to feel his lips and hands all over my body.

Stepping out of my pyjamas, I take a quick shower before I have to head downstairs, taking extra care with my new tattoo. Nerves are igniting my body as I think of seeing Sean this morning. Need is snaking down my spine in anticipation.

I wanted—no, needed—an escape from my life. The pressure to be perfect is too much. But with Sean? There is no pressure. I don't have to be the perfect princess. I can show my true self without having to worry if I'll be judged too harshly.

Not paying attention as I leave the flat, I run smack into a hard body at the end of the stairs.

"Mmm, morning, love." Sean's steadying hands grip my elbows so I don't fall backwards. A smile brightens his handsome face. It makes me weak in the knees.

"Good morning." There's a connection between us that we didn't have before last night. I had never given a second thought to getting a tattoo, even if the decision was made out of an angry reaction, but there's an intimacy involved in it. One that I feel wholeheartedly with Sean.

"How are you feeling this morning?" Sean tucks a loose strand of hair behind my ear. Even the casual touch sets me on fire.

"Happy." I return the smile.

"I'm glad to hear that, but I was asking about the tattoo. Any pain?"

My face burns with embarrassment. I can't be the only one feeling things after last night, can I? He was equally greedy in that kiss. Before my mind spins out of control, Sean gives me a lingering, chaste kiss. I lean into him as his lips leave mine.

"I should've led with that." Sean's eyes are alight with amusement. "But c'mon, I do want to see how your tattoo is doing." Taking me by the hand, he pulls me down the hall towards his office. I feel like a giddy schoolgirl with a crush.

Sean shuts the door behind me before taking a seat in his leather chair. Stepping between his legs, I sweep my pink hair to the side and lift my shirt. His warm hands hold me still on either side of the new artwork. The air crackles with electricity. A storm of emotion brews in my belly. I never want to forget the feel of his touch. It's more consuming than I've ever felt in my life. It should scare me how quickly this is happening, but the man who is holding me at his side is one of the most real people I've ever met.

"Why don't I put a little more cream on it for you? It's looking great." His thumb is rubbing slow circles just under my breast. Peering down at him, my eyes catch his and they are ablaze with heat. Dropping the side of my shirt, I push him back in the chair and straddle him.

"Can I get a proper good morning kiss first?" I'm loving this newfound courage that I seem to have found. Maybe it's the pink hair. Maybe it's that no one knows who I am. But Kat takes what she wants. And right now? I want Sean.

Sean answers by sealing his lips over mine, gentle at first, but then his tongue demands entrance. I feel powerful being over him, at feeling how turned on he is. His hands on my backside pull me closer into him. We barely fit on the chair, but there is no way I want to break this kiss.

The electricity sparks around us as we lose ourselves in each other. His hands in my hair, my hands running down his chest. His lips at my neck, nibbling along the sensitive flesh. My greedy moans give away just how much I want this kiss.

"Fuck, Kat. If we're not careful, I could take you right here. And that's not how I want to do things." His swollen lips and hooded eyes tell me how much he wants me. I know he felt the connection last night too.

"And how do you want to do things, Sean?" His hands move tenderly over me, like he wants to treat me with care.

"I want to take you out on a date tonight."

"I'll have to check my diary." A giggle slips out.

"Oh yeah?" He squeezes my backside, and I fight the groan as pleasure snakes through me.

"I might have another hot date tonight." I love the cheeky side that comes out when I'm with Sean.

"Need I remind you whose lap you're sitting on right now?" He squeezes me closer to him, and I hold him to my chest, resting my cheek on top of his head.

"A very handsome man."

I let the quiet wash over me for a moment. I never get to have moments like this with a man. It's usually a date at a restaurant and dodging the paparazzi. I have no idea what our date will consist of tonight, but I already know it will be the best one yet.

"Kat?" Sean's hot breath ghosts over me as my thoughts come back to where we are. I pull back, cupping his strong jaw in my hands. I don't know if I'll ever get my fix of this man.

"Tonight. But you have to pick me up after work. I need time to get ready."

"Love, I'll give you all the time you need." He gives me another kiss before moving me off of him. "Now, let me take care of your tattoo and then we've got a shop to run."

———

"SHOREDITCH INK. Kat speaking. How may I help you?" It's been a busy morning, but I love it. I've been sneaking peeks at Sean all morning. The other boys keep making kissing faces at us, but I couldn't care less.

"Hi, Kat. Is one of those precious Bond boys there?"

"Bond boys? I'm not sure who you want to speak with." The voice on the other end has a slight American accent, as if years of living in England has watered it down.

"Sean or Pierce? I was hoping to catch them before their dad and I leave for Amsterdam." Wheels start turning in my head as the voice on the other end of the line keeps talking.

"I'm sorry, but I'm new here. You're their mum? Sean and Pierce?"

"On the days they claim me. Are either of them around? They weren't picking up their phones."

"They're back in Sean's office. But back to this Bond boys business." My voice is dripping with excitement.

"Darling, you're British. You know who James Bond is."

"Absolutely I do. But why are they your Bond boys?"

"Oh, fuck." Sean's loud voice is behind me as I swivel to see him coming out of his office. "Kat, give me the phone."

"Oh, he sounds mad. Yes, dear. I named them both after James Bond actors. Growing up in America, I was in love with everything British and Bond. Who can help but swoon at those accents?"

"You are so right. Swoon-worthy indeed." The grin I'm giving Sean as he hovers over me is sparkling. "You have absolutely made my day. May I ask your name?"

"Jacquelyn. It's lovely to meet you, Kat."

I'm smirking at Sean and Pierce, not quite ready to hand the phone over. "It's lovely to meet you. Now, seeing as how I'm getting death glares from these Bond boys of yours, I'll hand the phone over."

Pierce grabs the phone from my hand as Sean hovers over me. Fisting his shirt, I pull him down closer. "James Bond, huh?"

He drops his head to my shoulder. "I really need to change the landline number."

"Oh no, you don't, Bond. I want your mum to ring here all the time." I can't keep the laughter out of my voice. "I love knowing that my sexy tattooist is named after the actor who portrayed one of the most iconic characters ever created."

"You don't have to be so excited." His lips at my ear send tingles rushing over my body.

"Oh, I am very excited. My very own James Bond. Will you take me somewhere tonight so we can have martinis?"

"Date is over before it even began." He pulls away and heads back over to his station.

"Hopefully it was good while it lasted, Bond."

He shakes his head. "Mum."

"See you at seven, Bond."

———

EVEN THOUGH IT was a busy afternoon at the shop, Sean let me leave early so I could pick up a few things for tonight. Not knowing what I would be doing while on my "holiday," I didn't pack date-appropriate clothing. Thankfully, I was able to pop into a local shop and find a simple dress.

Butterflies have taken up residence in my stomach as I apply the finishing touches on my hair and makeup. It's simple. I didn't want to overdo it. Finishing the braids in my hair, I twist them around my head and secure them in place. The black dress I found stands out against my pink hair. I've gotten so used to looking in the mirror and seeing pink. It's fun. It's bright. It's so far out of my comfort zone that I love it. I'll never get to have this again, so I'm enjoying it while I can.

A soft knock at the door quells all thoughts in my head. I've never been more excited for a first date before. And with Sean? The nerves are fighting for control. I want everything to be perfect. Taking a deep breath, I walk over to the door and open it. The sexiest man I've ever seen is awaiting me, in dark jeans hugging his thighs and a white shirt with the sleeves rolled up, exposing his tattoos. He's droolworthy. How did I get so lucky to find this man?

"Wow, Kat. Just wow." Grabbing my hand, he holds me at arm's length, his gaze lazily taking me in. I give him a quick spin, the skirt of my simple T-shirt dress floating around my legs.

"Stunning. Absolutely stunning."

"I can say the same about you." I drink in the man in front of me. The tattoos, the rolled sleeves...it all adds up to a man I am undoubtedly falling for. "So where are you taking me, Bond?"

Sean just shakes his head at me. "You think you're so funny, don't you?"

Wrapping my arms around his waist, I pull him closer to me, a grin plastered over my face. "I'm hilarious, and you love it."

"Whatever you say, Kat. Now, let's get going because otherwise, we won't make it out tonight."

———

SEAN

Christ. I've never seen such a beautiful woman in my entire life. I wasn't prepared for Kat when she opened the door, standing there in that dress.

Legs for days.

Curves I want to feel under my hands.

Hair in an elaborate updo.

And those lips. I can't wait to taste them again.

"You're staring." Kat's voice breaks me out of my obvious perusal.

"It's hard not to when you're so damn sexy." A blush creeps up her neck at my words as she pushes me out the door.

There is a low hum of activity on the street as we head out the back door. It's a rare, perfect spring night in London. Just what I wanted for tonight.

"So, where are you taking me?" Kat asks again, lacing her fingers through mine. It's an instant shock to the system. I felt it the day she walked into my shop and it's only gotten stronger.

"You are not one for surprises, are you?" I look down at her. Her light blue eyes are happy as they gaze up at me.

"Let's just say my life is usually very well planned. I know where I'll be every day for months on end. So it's hard not to know."

I give her a curious stare. She is tight-lipped, revealing very little to me. "Maybe it'll do you some good, love, to not know."

"As long as you're my guide this evening, I'll be very happy." She rests her head on my shoulder as we quietly wander in the direction I've planned for us this evening. It's a comfortable silence as we enjoy the street art on our walk. I always want to fill the silence, but with Kat, it's different. I can feel her head moving as she takes in the street art that surrounds us.

"Is this why you decided to open a shop in Shore-ditch?" Her eyes are trained on the intricate roses painted on the front of a building ahead of us. They are on fire in the evening sun.

"Because of all the art?"

She nods her head. "Maybe you could paint these roses on me next." She drops my hand and moves to the building, tracing the outline of the flowers on the wall.

"Why don't you let the first one heal and then we'll talk seconds." Let's be honest, there's no way I would deny this woman anything. She's taken a firm hold of me and hasn't let go.

"I think I'm healing quite nicely. Maybe in a few weeks, I can have something on my other side."

"Whatever you want, love." I wrap my arms around her waist and turn her to me. She looks like an angel in the sunlight. I catch her lips with mine. They move gently beneath mine, as we stand in the spotlight of the sun on a crowded London street.

We stay like this, wrapped up in each other for who knows how long. It isn't until someone bumps into me from behind that we pull away from each other. Kat's eyes are closed as she holds on to me, her lips swollen from our kiss.

"I think we should head to dinner." Brushing my knuckles over her cheek, I drop a kiss to her forehead before we continue down the pavement. Kat's hands wrap around my arm as we walk. Her fingers move up and down my exposed forearm.

"You know, I might have a few ideas for this arm." Her voice is filled with amusement as she continues tracing the veins on my forearm. Her touch lights me up from the inside out. I can't get enough of it.

"Oh yeah?"

She nods her head gently against me. "Maybe you could have a pink-haired woman on your arm."

I bark out a laugh. "Sorry, love. You know the rules."

"I know. No faces or names."

"You're a fast learner. Here we are." I swing her attention to the old brick building in front of us. She stops and gives me a skeptical look.

"A pub? Really?"

"Don't give me that look." Her hands are on her hips as she pierces me with her most withering stare. "It's not just a pub. C'mon. You'll love it."

She shakes her head at me as I take her hand in mine, leading her inside the old building. There's restaurants and event space all around us, but the real highlight is out back.

"Wow. This is incredible." Kat's voice is full of awe as I push open the old metal door. The large outdoor space has picnic tables set up all around. Food trucks and bars line the space. Strands of old lights cross the patio, glittering back at me in Kat's wide eyes. She looks fecking gorgeous.

"Told you it's not just a pub." Wrapping my hands around her waist, I guide her in front of me towards the food area. Asian, Caribbean, burgers. You name it, this place has it.

"What'll it be, love?" I whisper in her ear.

She turns back to look up at me, her face bright with excitement. "How about a little of everything?"

"Coming right up."

———

"THIS MIGHT BE some of the most delicious food I've ever had." Tucked into a quiet corner in the back, Kat's leaning against me ever so slightly. Empty trays of food are scattered in front of us.

"Truman's is one of my favourites." I take a long drink of my beer, setting it down and facing Kat. "It always changes, so you never know what you're going to get."

"Maybe you'll have to bring me back then to see what else they have."

"Pretty cocky there thinking this is going well, love." I love that she's already thinking about a second date. I'm thinking well beyond that.

"I didn't scare you off that first night at the pub." Her cheeks redden at the memory. "And I'm pretty sure I'm going to get a goodnight kiss tonight. So yes, I'm planning ahead."

"Plan away."

Soft, slow music starts to drift around us, and Kat's face lights up. I look around and see that couples are starting to make their way to a makeshift dance floor. I don't even need her to ask to know what she wants.

"Dance with me." She's biting down on her bottom lip in anticipation of my answer. I'm not sure there's anything I could deny her. It should scare me, the intensity of my feelings for her, but it doesn't.

Standing, I drop my hand to pull her up from the table. Her eyes beam with happiness as we walk over to the dance floor. Couples are moving quietly around us as I take Kat in my arms.

The air is thick with heat as I gently move us to the rhythm. I don't recognize the song, but it doesn't matter. The feel of Kat's curves under my hands, her arms wrapped around me as she hums along to the song, is indescribable. I'm trying to stay cool, but my heart could beat out of my chest right now. There's no keeping it cool with Kat.

Running my hands up her back, I cup her head in my

hands and turn her to look at me. Pools of blue are swimming with emotion as I take her lips with mine.

It's the most sensual kiss of my life. I don't care that we're surrounded by people. I lick the seam of her lips, and she immediately opens to me. Her hands are bruising on my back as I deepen the kiss. I swallow the moans as I pull her closer to me.

I can't get enough of this woman. She came storming into my shop, and now it's hard to imagine my life without this pink-haired goddess. Christ, I'm well and truly fucked, aren't I?

Chapter Eleven

KAT

For a Friday night, it's slow. There's usually more walk-ins at this time, or so I'm told. Trevor has been working on someone for the last hour or so, but other than that, it's been quiet. Pierce and Sean disappeared into his office a little bit ago, leaving me out here on my own.

I try distracting myself by reading my book, but my brain keeps going back to Sean and our date last night. It was like nothing I'd ever experienced in my life. It was simple, but perfect. Instead of trying to impress me with the latest Michelin-starred restaurant, Sean had known exactly what I needed. He took me to a local spot he knew I would like. And that soul-searching kiss at the end? It kept me up most of the night. My face gets hot still thinking about it.

"Oy! Princess, are you listening to me?" Fingers snapping in front of my face cause a panic to spread through me. A larger man is standing in front of the desk with two friends behind him. His glassy eyes and pungent smell mean he must have staggered in from the pub down the street.

"I'm sorry. May I help you?" I try to keep my voice even. There's no way this man knows who I am, but it's rattled me. Whatever this thing Sean and I have, it's new. Too fresh for a secret of this size to come to light right now.

"Yeah, I want a tattoo." Years of training to deal with the press keeps my face unchanged at this mess of a man in front of me. My eyes shift to Trevor, who is now watching the exchange closely.

"Do you have something in mind?" There is no way anyone will give this man a tattoo tonight. He's bloody pissed from one too many at the pub.

His eyes move over my chest in a lecherous way. "Maybe I can get you to give me this tattoo."

"Well, that's impossible. That's not something I do."

"That's a shame. I'd pay good money to have your hands on me." He licks his lips, as if that would entice me. I'm done with this creep of a man. His friends are snickering behind him. Men...if you can even call these boys that.

"Sorry, but no one is going to be tattooing you tonight. Come back tomorrow when you're sober."

"That's no way to treat a paying customer, princess."

"Seeing as how you're not a paying customer, I can treat you any way I want. Now you need to leave. Right now." He staggers back slightly, as if he can't believe he's being told off by a woman. Trevor is now standing, his arms crossed in a menacing manner.

His eyes drift behind me as he asks, "Are you going to let her treat me like this?"

"Damn straight. Now get the hell out of my shop and don't come back." Sean's voice as he steps out of his office is deep and growly. Turning to face him, I'm shocked I don't see smoke coming out of his ears. The jingle of the bell tells me the three idiots have left.

"My office." Sean turns and stalks off. Trevor whistles as I go to follow.

"Damn. I don't think I've ever seen him so pissed." I give him a quick look before following after Sean.

I don't know what that man was hoping to get out of here tonight, but clearly that wasn't what he wanted.

I'm not the meek little princess anymore. No, I'm standing up for myself like I've always wanted to. And that makes me feel like a badass.

Sean is on me before I even close the door. His hands fist in my hair and his lips crash down on mine. His tongue demands entry into my mouth, and I grant him access.

This kiss is hot. It's possessive. It's everything a kiss should be. Fisting my hands in his shirt, I pull him into my chest, feeling his hard muscles under my hand. And, oh God, I can feel his erection digging into me.

"Sean." My voice is lust-filled as he kisses down my neck.

"Kat. That was the fecking hottest thing I've ever witnessed in my life."

Sean nibbles on my bottom lip, tugging it between his teeth. I've never been more turned on in my life.

"What, me putting him in his place?" My hips move on their own, seeking out the heat from the growing bulge in his pants.

"Yes. I heard them come in, but clearly you don't need anyone's help taking care of things."

The confidence he has in me surges through my veins. It feels good to not be the compliant little princess. I'm not doing exactly what is told of me. No. I'm standing up for myself and telling people off. And it feels fucking amazing.

Pushing up on my tiptoes, I seek out Sean's mouth. My hand moves to his backside, squeezing him closer to me.

"We need to take this upstairs, love. I don't want our first time to be on my desk."

"Mmm, maybe we can save the desk for next time," I whisper in his ear.

"I like the way you think. Now, upstairs." He spins me around to face the door, slapping my backside as we go to the flat.

The moment the door closes behind me, my earlier confidence starts to fade. Every rude whisper and snarky comment about my body battles for dominance in my head. I want to stay in the moment with Sean, but it's hard when I'm battling my own inner turmoil.

Sean pins me against the door as he flicks the light switch on. His lips never leave my neck.

I flick the light switch off before Sean turns it back on. "Off," I whisper against his lips. He pulls back, his face drawn in confusion.

"I want to see you. I want to see your face when you come. When you're turned on to the point you might explode."

My skin feels tight as I walk over to the window. It's embarrassing to have to tell someone you want to sleep with that you hate how you look. Everyone always says to have a thick skin, but when the media rips apart your appearance every chance they get, it's hard.

"What's wrong, love?" That heat from his body is a welcome distraction behind me.

"I just…" I sigh, turning to face him. I know my own cheeks are probably red with embarrassment. "It's just…I don't want you to see me, you know, naked."

He rears back, as if I slapped him. "You know that's hard to do when you're having sex, right?"

Fisting my hands in his shirt, I keep him at a distance. "When your appearance is judged, and judged harshly, it starts to seep in that you are not worthy based on how you look." My voice is quiet as I stare at my hands. His fingers tilt my chin up to meet his gaze. Anger and lust swirl in the depths of his icy blue eyes.

"Who is telling you this?"

I shrug. "People."

"These people are arseholes. Shitheads. You are the sexiest woman I have ever laid eyes on, and I can't wait to feel these curves without clothes in the way." As if to prove his point, his hands slide around my back, dipping under my shirt. "I'll let you have no lights tonight. But I am going to devour you. I am going to kiss every inch of your skin and tell you why I love it. And when we're done, you'll have no doubts as to who is the sexiest woman in the universe."

His lips crash down on mine and I can only hold on for dear life. As his hands move around to my backside to lift me up, I don't think about how everyone says it's oversized peaches. All I can think about is how good his tongue feels against mine. About how good him squeezing said backside feels. And, oh God, how good his erection feels against my core.

Sean sets me down on the bed in front of him, the glow of the streetlamps making him look devastatingly handsome. I grab the hem of his shirt and pull him down over me, while tugging the shirt over his head. The ink on his skin dances in front of me. I've never been with anyone before who has tattoos. But the contrast of colours against his skin is sinfully sexy. For once, I don't have to hide my perusal of his body. My fingers lightly trace the patterns that are intricately decorating his chest.

Sean grabs my fingers and brings them to his lips. "If

you keep doing that, love, this is going to be over real fast. Embarrassingly fast." I can't hide the smile that brightens my face as I lay back on the bed. Heat and nerves fight for control over my body, as Sean's gaze travels from head to toe.

"Get out of your head, Kat." His hot breath ghosts over my lips as he kisses his way down my jaw to my ear. His heavy weight settles over me, keeping me in the moment.

"Want to know what I like about your neck?"

"What?" My voice is full of lust as it escapes in a long breath.

"I like how you stretch it when you've had a long day. All this exposed flesh just begging for my teeth." He nibbles his way down my neck, licking the sting away as he goes. Heat coils tight in my core as Sean's hands push my shirt farther and farther up.

"Tell me more."

Sean's face is directly over mine as he tugs my shirt up and over my head.

"I like the sound of your voice." His lips are back on my neck. "I like how breathy it is. I like how happy it is when you're at the shop." His lips are at the top of my breasts. I suck in a deep breath as he pulls one of the cups down, exposing a taut nipple, ripe for the taking.

"I like that I cause this reaction in you." Sean's mouth covers my nipple, taking it between his teeth and giving it a hearty pull.

"Oh my God!" My back arches off the bed, wanting to be closer to Sean.

"Do you even know how bloody gorgeous you look in those shirts you wear?" Sean kisses his way to my other breast, giving it the same treatment. "These tits. Fuck, I've wanted to have my hands on them every day." Sean sits up, taking my full breasts into his hands, rubbing his thumbs over my nipples.

Reaching behind me, I unsnap my bra and fling it off. Sean's hands move farther down my stomach, resting on my waist. Biting down on my lip, I close my eyes. I'm not ready to hear his reaction to my fuller sides. Or not hear any reaction at all.

"Eyes on me, Kat." My eyes open to see his are on mine. They are full of lust and passion. I couldn't look away if I tried.

"Sean, I—" He cuts me off with a searing kiss, his tongue tangling with mine. He pulls back ever so slightly and my lips chase his.

"No. These curves. You're one of the sexiest women I've ever seen. Do you know what I felt when I had them under my hands when I was inking you?"

I shake my head in response.

"I thought I was the luckiest bastard in the world to get to see you so vulnerable. To hear your story of why this tattoo means something to you." His fingers trace the still sensitive flowers on my side. "I love what I do, but getting to do it for you was a privilege."

My heart starts to flutter. Sean's hands move over my curves with a reverence I've never felt. Those lips I love so much move over my curves, curves that normally cause me so much pain. But right now? I feel like a sex goddess pulling my man in with my siren song.

My core is aching for relief. Sean's hands deftly undo the button and zipper of my jeans and he slowly works them over my hips and thighs. "And fuck...these thighs, Kat. I can't wait to have them wrapped around my head as I make you come all over my tongue."

"Yes! Sean, I need your mouth on me now." My voice comes out on a moan, as I'm now laid out in just my thong before him. His hands are rubbing up and down my legs, like he can't get enough of my curves.

"I haven't had my fill of you yet. Of just how beautiful you are." Goose pimples break out all over my skin as his warm hands move up and down my legs. The bulge in his jeans shows just how much I affect him. And I love it.

This time, when his hands skate over my legs, they continue to the apex of my thighs. His thumbs brush ever so lightly over my dripping core as he slides my thong down my legs and off. It's an explosion of heat and fire as I try to quell the storm of emotions racing through me. Sean's lips come down on my hip bone, gently tugging the skin between his teeth.

"I'm going to mark every inch of your skin as my own. You're mine, Kat." God, it's sexy to have him want to brand me like this. Coming from anyone else, it would grate on me. But from Sean? It makes me feel treasured. Worshipped.

I push that errant thought out of my head. It's too early to be feeling these emotions. But when Sean's lips finally land where I want them, every thought is pushed from my mind. His tongue is pure magic as it traces up and down my slit.

"You're so ready for me, Kat."

"Uh-huh." My fingers thread through his hair as I clutch him to me. I don't want his mouth to move from my pussy. As he slides one finger into my heated channel, his lips suck down on my clit, and he teases it with his tongue.

"Sean! Oh, yes! Right there!" My legs close tighter around his head as he drives me closer and closer to orgasm. Sean adds a second finger as he starts pumping faster and faster. The orgasm barrels through me as I come on a shout. Technicolour stars burst behind my eyes as I ride Sean's face through an earth-shattering orgasm. Pleasure courses through my entire body, from the top of my head to the tips of my toes.

Sean's hands on my legs bring me out of my post-orgasm bliss. His lips are wet with my release as I pull him up to me. Capturing his lips with mine, I moan in delight as I taste myself on him. Distracting him with a soul-searing kiss, I flip us over so I'm on top of him.

"It's my turn to worship your body."

"Mmm, worship away, love." I kiss my way down his body, mirroring the attention he was giving to me only moments ago. But when I come to the tattoos on his chest, I lick the intricate patterns. I smile against his skin as I feel his hard cock beneath me. "Christ, Kat. That feels amazing."

My fingers and lips move lower as the ink disappears into the waistband of his jeans. Making quick work of his belt, I lower his jeans, leaving him in just his boxer briefs. Sean kicks his jeans to the side as I take his cock out. It's the perfect size. Giving it a few pumps, I move my lips over the head, swiping the bead of precum from the slit. Sean's hips move on their own, thrusting into my mouth. I moan and hum as I start pulling him deeper. I savor the taste of him as I move over the velvet iron of his cock.

"Kat. I need to be inside you. Now." His voice is growly as he pulls me up and over him. "Rubbers are in the pocket of my jeans."

"Really?"

"Figured I'd stock up. Just in case."

"Such an optimist." I drop a chaste kiss on his lips as I lean over to grab a rubber while he pulls the boxer briefs the rest of the way off. Ripping it open, I deftly roll it down his erection. He tries to pull me back under him, but I push him down. Any lingering doubts about my body were blasted out with the orgasm to end all orgasms.

With each pass of his tongue and lips over mine, he tore down my walls. I don't want to hide my body. Not from him. I want to put it on display where he can worship it. Settling over him, I line myself up and sink down onto him.

"Fuck." Sean's voice slips out on a hiss as I still over him. My nails drag down his chest as I adjust to his size filling me. Sean's calloused hands rub up and down my thighs. A slight squeeze brings my gaze down to his.

Locking eyes with him, I start to move. Every roll and grind amps my pleasure to new heights. Heights that I am already looking back on after my previous orgasm. Sean's hands move higher, brushing over my clit as heat swirls between the two of us.

I've never felt so powerful and in control as I do now. Heat and desire are etched on his face as he leans up to take a nipple in his mouth. The long locks of my hair caress my backside as my head is thrown back in pleasure.

"I'm going to come again. Oh my God!" I shout as I tumble over the edge. Sean holds me tight to his chest as he continues thrusting into me. The world could be imploding around us, but as Sean comes on a final thrust, everything fades into the background. It's just him and me in this small flat, tucked away in London. There's no pressure to look or act a certain way. Just the two of us, holding onto one another like we never want to let go.

His breath is hot on my neck as we cling to one another, not moving, our skin slick. My body is liquid. I never want to move from this spot, with Sean underneath me and his arms holding me tight.

"Christ, Kat. That was fecking amazing."

"Eh, I give it a seven." Sean flips us over, his cock already growing hard inside me.

"Seven, eh? Are you just trying to get another round in?" His eyes are playful.

"I don't know. You'll just have to prove your worth, Bond."

Chapter Twelve

KAT

The early morning sun streaming in the room stirs me awake. My body aches in the best possible way. I've never had a night like I did last night. The men I'd been with were mediocre at best. When with a royal, one must sign a non-disclosure agreement before taking one's clothes off. But last night there wasn't even the thought of an NDA. It was all passion and lust. Only teeth and tongues and lips and our bodies moving together.

The lazy smile on my face is happy, despite the bed being cold beside me, and I finally get the energy to sit up. Sean's in the kitchen, wearing nothing but sweatpants that hang low on his hips, exposing the sexy ink covering his back. Finding his shirt, I slip it on and walk over to him in the small flat.

"Morning." My voice is gravelly as I wrap my arms around his waist and drop a kiss to his back.

"Mmm, morning, love." Sean's hands cover mine before he turns and pulls me into his chest. "I hope you're hungry. I'm making bangers and mash."

"I'm one lucky girl. No one has ever made me such a spread before."

"Then no one has been deserving of you." He drops a soft kiss on my lips before pulling back. On instinct, I wrap my hand around his head and pull him back down. I don't want to lose contact just yet. He tastes like mint and tea, the perfect morning combination.

"This is all very James Bond of you. Wooing your girl with breakfast." Hopping up on the counter, I grab his tea and take my own sip. My ogling is obvious as he continues making breakfast. Is there anything sexier than a man cooking? The way his bicep flexes as he mixes everything is droolworthy. Very unbecoming of a princess.

"If making you breakfast woos you, I'll happily make it for you every day of the week." The cheeky smile on his face sends sparks straight to my toes. I hide my own smile behind the cup of tea as Sean plates our breakfast.

Instead of going to the small table, we stay where we are. The smell is divine. Usually, breakfast consists of yogurt or oatmeal before I'm off to another event. But the sausage and mash is the perfect morning pick-me-up.

"Stop your staring, love. I still have to open the shop, and if you're lucky, you might get to join me in the shower."

"Well then, this sounds like the perfect morning."

———

"DO we really need to go to work?" I'm wrapped in a towel as Sean finishes getting dressed. "Don't you want to stay in bed with me all day?"

"Love, there is nothing I want more than to stay right here with you. But just think. It will make tonight even better." He comes over to me, his hands diving under the towel. The warmth of his hands at my waist heats my entire body. His lips ghost over mine.

"Now, get dressed and come downstairs. Maybe I'll take you out for a long lunch."

"Tease."

"Don't be late. Hate to dock your pay." Sean turns and leaves, a playful smile on his face. He just gave me another amazing orgasm in the shower, and watching him leave causes a burning need to wash through me. I don't know how I'll ever get my fill of this man.

I grab the first thing I can find in the dresser. Sean still had clothes here for late nights at work, and I throw on one of his shirts and tie it at the waist. It will drive him wild today, and I want to torment him as much as he was tormenting me earlier.

Throwing my hair into a messy bun, I head downstairs. It's quiet, still not opening time. But as I turn the corner, three sets of eyes stare me down.

"Well, well, well. Look who's finally here." Ruby's face sparkles with excitement, while Trevor and Pierce stare back at her.

"It's ten in the morning, Ruby."

"And I expected you to stay upstairs much longer."

"What in the world are you talking about?" Pierce and Trevor share a confused look.

"Guys. We open in thirty minutes. Let's get rolling." Sean's eyes land on me as everyone leaves the back area. His eyes are black with desire as they scan my attire.

"What in the world are you wearing?" I love the way his hands wrap around me, holding me close to him.

"Well, you wouldn't let us stay in bed today, so I had to have a part of you with me." I give him the most innocent of looks.

"You don't play fair." His lips suck down on the spot behind my ear. I'm purring with delight.

"And neither do you. Now, I do believe you said it's time to go to work." Giving his backside a firm squeeze, I leave him hanging.

"You're going to pay for that, Kat."

I turn back and give him my sultriest look. "Looking forward to it."

———

"SO, HOW WAS LAST NIGHT?" Ruby brought lunch for everyone but told the men to stay up front. "We need girl time," she said.

"Just your standard night at the shop. Why do you ask?" Sipping my drink, I give her a coy look.

"Trevor said Sean was ready to murder those blokes who came in the shop. But then he never saw either of you again."

My face heats at the memory. There was a hunger between the two of us that I've never felt before. The raw need was palpable.

"If you saw us, it would've been quite the scandal."

"Is he as good in bed as he looks? Christ, don't tell Trevor I asked that. But the men in this store are their own specimen of fine."

"Truer words have never been spoken, Ruby. It was fantastic." The way he worshipped me, kissed me, laved attention on me…it was out of this world.

"Best shag of your life?"

"Without a doubt," I answer without pause. "But you are not to tell him that!"

She throws her hands up. "Girl code. Whatever you say stays between the two of us."

I blush at her words. I've never had a good friend like her. It was always hard to make friends growing up. You never knew if someone wanted genuine friendship or something from you because of your position.

But Ruby is one of the most genuine people I've met. I was welcomed into her world after knowing her for all of five minutes. My mind keeps drifting to when I'll be back at the palace in just a short time. I can't imagine my life without these people in it.

"Now, enough talk about these boys. I want you to help me design my new tattoo."

Chapter Thirteen

KAT

It's a perfect day. It's been gloomier than usual lately, with no sun in sight. But on this rare, sunny day, I dragged Sean with me to the park. It's packed with families and small children, no doubt needing to get out and enjoy the day.

And what an enjoyable day it is. Sean's head is resting in my lap while I read. I can't remember the last time I've read for fun. Usually after a long day of scheduled events, I'm too tired to do anything but fall into bed. But sitting here in the park with Sean, it couldn't get any better than this.

It's the kind of perfect day that might not be in my future. It's getting closer and closer to when my holiday is supposed to end. An ache I've never known settles over me every time I think about leaving this place. About leaving Sean. I can't imagine going back to the palace and having every minute of my life scheduled. Having every move, every look picked apart. It's panic-inducing.

"Where'd you go, love?" Sean's voice brings me back to

the present. My fingers have been stroking his hair, loving the silky feel.

"Just thinking about you." It isn't an outright lie, but I don't really want to get into the truth now. How does one go about telling someone they are falling for that they aren't who they say they are?

"Hopefully good things," he says, leaning up and capturing my lips with his. The taste of the beer he had with lunch lingers on his lips.

"Like how I have my very own James Bond and all the wicked things I want to do to him."

"Oh, I do like these things. I don't know why we're lazing around here when we could be going at it in bed." His eyes are telling. He's ready to bolt and make good on his word. And while it wouldn't be the worst way to spend the afternoon, I shove him right back down.

"Cool it, Bond. We're taking advantage of this day. I could use some sunshine." Usually getting sunshine means tucking myself away in a corner of my garden where I can't be seen. But being out here in the park where no one knows who I am is the most incredible feeling in the world. "I want to get back to reading, so you hush."

"And what are you reading, love?" His eyes are closed again as my hand drifts under the V of his T-shirt. I've memorized the patterns of ink that mark his skin.

"A romance book." It was too tempting to pass up at the corner market when I was getting my escape items. I never get to read for pleasure, and the half-naked man on the front was very enticing.

"And what kind of romance book?" His hand comes down on top of mine, stilling my motion. The beat of his heart under my palm keeps me settled.

"Historical. A lady is betrothed to a duke whom she

does not love. She is secretly in love with a duke from a neighboring village, and their villages are feuding."

"Sounds very British."

"Very much so. And the sex scenes are rather good."

"Oh yeah?"

"Yes."

"Tell me about them." His voice is deep, full of desire. It shouldn't be such a turn-on to tell him about my book, but it sends shockwaves through my body.

"Well, the lady runs away in defiance of her parents. She doesn't want to be forced into a loveless marriage. It causes a big to-do in her tiny village, but she stays with her duke. The one she loves."

"She's quite feisty, this lady. Like someone else I know." He squeezes my hand but doesn't let go.

"Quite. She ends up marrying the duke she loves, and it causes a fight to break out. But they can't help the passion they feel for one another. Their desire and love are all-consuming."

His eyes are now on me, his lips parted, as if I could read him the entire story and he would be enraptured.

"Their lovemaking is incredibly sensual."

"Describe it to me."

His heart is racing under my hand as his gaze stays fixed on mine. I couldn't look away if I wanted to.

"She sneaks into his room—"

He cuts me off. "Why aren't they sleeping together?"

"The men and women slept in separate rooms back then."

"I'm glad we changed with the times. I don't want you sleeping anywhere but next to me." Thank God I'm sitting, because this man is absolutely swoon-worthy.

"Yes, times have indeed changed. The lady is only in her dressing gown when she finds her love. He is still awake, drinking whisky, sitting in front of the fire. She is terribly in love with him. She has never been with another man before, but she cannot wait to be with him." I know the feeling. Being around Sean, my body is always in tune with where he is. It's as if there's an invisible thread locking the two of us together.

"Instead of her dropping her clothes, the duke removes his pants, standing in just his riding shirt. He's already hard in anticipation." Just saying this out loud to Sean feels indecent, as we're surrounded by families in the park. But I can't seem to stop myself from continuing. Heat and fire are coursing through my veins. It's as if Sean and I are the duke and the new duchess.

"She goes to him, ready to give herself over. They've barely shared a kiss before now, but she's ready to be his in every sense of the word."

Sean sits up in a flash, pulling my chest to his. My nipples are hard beneath the fabric of my thin T-shirt. His hand goes to my hair as his mouth whispers next to my ear.

"What happens next?"

"He shoves her dressing gown up and slowly, oh so slowly, slides into her." His voice is a growl as he starts nibbling on my neck. Never have I been a part of something so erotic.

"He doesn't rip it off of her? I wouldn't be able to wait to see her naked beneath me."

"He is still a gentleman. They make mad, passionate love. She gives him something precious to her, and he vows to protect her with whatever comes next."

Sean's lips crash down on mine in a fervent kiss, filled with desire and passion. His tongue slides against mine in a fight for control. I've never been more turned on in my life. I can't keep my hands off of him as we sit in the park and kiss like our lives depend on it. The heat swirling between the two of us is palpable. The sounds of London drift off into the background as Sean starts working his way down my neck. I'm about to tell him we need to stop when the first drop hits me square in the face.

Opening my eyes, I realize that the sun is gone and storm clouds have moved in. We were so distracted that the entire world was fuzzy around us. Everyone else has run for shelter as we're the last ones in the park.

"Shit!" Sean yells as the skies open up. We barely have time to pack everything up before we're dashing through the park, trying to make it to safety. Finding a tree, we grab what little cover we can while trying to get things organised before leaving.

"Hey." Sean grabs me and pulls me towards him, causing me to drop the few things I have in my hands. His T-shirt sticks to his muscles, showing off his powerful chest. I pull his head down to me, not wanting to leave this spot. Our kiss is just as heated as it was before the heavens opened up. I pull his bottom lip between my teeth, loving the growl that hits my ear.

"Don't think just because it started raining, I'm done with you." He leans closer to me, whispering in my ear. His hands pull me in closer so I can feel the heat of his hard body. "Don't think that duke has anything on what I plan on doing to you when we get home."

———

THE HALLWAY IS quiet as we rush into the back of the shop to get out of the rain. The buzz of the tattoo guns is softer back here. Instead of going upstairs to the studio, Sean is crowding me from behind.

"Do you realize how sexy you look wet?" He brushes

the tangle of my hair to the side as his lips find my neck. Oh God, I love it when he sucks where my shoulder and neck meet.

"I have a feeling you'll tell me." I love Sean's hands. They are all over me as he works my shirt up and over my head. The groan that slips out is needy and full of desire. A slap to the ass brings me out of my thoughts. I don't think I've ever been more aroused in my entire life.

"You're a fucking wet dream, and I've been dying to take you all afternoon. Much like the duke." His breath ghosts my ear. "Now, we need to be quiet. Otherwise, someone out front will hear us, and I'll have to punish you."

I turn to peek at him. "Promise?"

He growls, ever so softly, and attacks my lips again. The snick of the zipper echoes loudly in the hallway as Sean tugs my pants down my legs.

"Fuck, are you not wearing underwear, love?" I turn, wiggling my arse in his direction as he trails hot, open-mouthed kisses down my back.

"Trying something new." The sting of a bite on my backside causes a rush of heat to gather in my core.

"You drive me wild." His tongue licks my slit as I hold myself up for dear life. The movement of his tongue and those nimble hands of his squeezing my arse is lighting me up from the inside out. I cover my mouth, moaning into my hand as he drives me closer and closer to bliss. Just when I think he's going to let me come, he's gone. I can't hide my whimpers of displeasure as I rub my legs together, needing some friction.

"Uh-uh. That's my job." Before I know it, I hear the sound of a foil packet opening, and then he slides his cock between my legs.

"Oh, God." I throw my head back, meeting his hard

chest. He fists my hair, pulling my head to the side. Soft kisses on the slope of my neck have me rocking my hips over his cock. "I could come just like this." My voice is a breathy whisper. The thought that anyone could come back here and find us has me rocketing back towards the edge.

"As much as I would like to try that, I want you coming all over my cock." Slowly, too slowly, he slides inside me until I'm so full I couldn't possibly take anymore. Sean places my hands on the wall before he slides out, finding a rhythm that has me convulsing with need.

I bite my lip to keep my moans to myself. Every time with Sean is better than the last. My senses are overwhelmed—the feel of him as he slides in and out of my slick channel, the sound of his belt clanking in the empty hallway, the taste of him on my lips. I need more.

Pulling a hand off the wall, I find his hair and tug him towards me, capturing his lips with mine. It's a fight for power as our tongues tangle. His free hand dips low on my body, finding my clit. I grab ahold, our fingers working me over together. Sean knows just how to play me to drive my pleasure to new heights.

"Close. So close," I whisper against his lips. He sucks my bottom lip into his mouth and he picks up the pace of his thrusts.

"Was it like this in your book?" Thrust. "The duke and his lady fucking in hidden corners?" Thrust. Thrust. "I don't know how much longer I can hold back, love." Thrust. "I'm going to need you to come."

And I do. I explode around him in a cacophony of colours and lights and stars. Fireworks as bright as the New Year's sky light me up from the inside out. I don't know how loud I'm being, but my entire body is awash in new feelings as Sean's own orgasm starts to sweep over him.

His hands are digging into my sides, keeping us both upright as we come down from the best high I've ever known. Sean's lips kiss up my neck, working over my jaw before lightly kissing my lips, gentle and easy compared to the fast and furious pace of what we just did in the hallway.

This isn't something a princess should be caught doing. Ever. It would devastate the monarchy in the worst way. But right now? I couldn't care less. I just had the best sex of my life with the best man I've ever met, and I'm in heaven.

He slowly pulls out, and I lament the loss of him. He ties off the condom before pulling his jeans, and then mine, back up. I turn to face him, standing in only my bra and jeans. His eyes are heavy in his post-orgasmic state. He's never looked sexier.

Lifting me into his arms, he presses me against the wall by the stairs. "I guess I'll need to punish you now."

"I was quiet." I didn't know if I was quiet. The world could have ended, and I would have been none the wiser.

"I'm surprised no one came back here. The whole of London probably heard you after that orgasm."

"Well, if you rock my world again like that, then by all means, take me to the tower and punish away."

The hungry gleam in his eyes tells me that's exactly what we'll be doing for the rest of the day.

Chapter Fourteen

SEAN

"Wake up, Kat." She barely stirs next to me. I shouldn't be all that surprised considering how late we stayed up. We're insatiable. I can't remember the last time I've had so much fun with a woman. I'm doing things I never thought I'd be doing with Kat. Her wide-eyed innocence makes me want to run off and leave all responsibilities behind.

"It's too early to get up." Her voice is muffled by the pillow. Her pink hair is practically glowing in the late morning sun. She looks like a dirty angel, lying here with her back exposed. Her side is no longer an angry red from her tattoo. It's healed nicely. I'm ready for the next tattoo. Ready to move my hands over her skin, inking her. It makes my dick stir. But we don't have time for that.

"It's almost noon." My voice is a whisper behind her ear as I gently run my fingertips up and down her spine.

"Noon?" She shoots up onto her elbows. Creases mar the side of her beautiful face. Fuck, this woman has burrowed her way into my heart.

"We were up late, love." I brush the silky locks of her

hair behind her ear and draw her lips into mine, morning breath be damned.

"Mmm, I do remember." She stretches before flipping onto her back, the sheet falling to expose those gorgeous tits I love.

"Kat. You really do need to get up. I have a fun day for us planned."

"We could have a fun day here instead." Her voice is still sleepy as she tries to pull me on top of her. As much as I don't want to resist her, I know she'll enjoy what I have planned.

"If it was up to you, we'd never leave this bed."

"And that's a problem because?" Her fingers trace the tattoos on my arm. She does this to distract me, but I'm on a mission to enjoy this day with her.

"As much as I would love to stay here with you in bed, I think you'll enjoy this too."

"Spoilsport." She throws the sheet off and stalks off, naked as the day she was born. I'm starting to question my own sanity by not staying in bed with her.

"Christ, Kat. Way to tease a man." She shakes her ass at me as she makes her way over to the bathroom.

"Maybe you could make it a quickie before we go?" She disappears behind the door, and I'm out of the bed and dropping my joggers before she can even turn the water on.

———

"ARE you going to tell me where we're going?" We got a later start than I had planned, but it was worth it for the mind-blowing sex in the shower. No man will ever complain about that.

"You'll see once we get there. I hope I'm not overselling it." Ever since we went to the pub, she wanted to go back and try others. I didn't quite see the appeal, but something about her enthusiasm made me want to bring her here.

"Sean." She stops and pulls me back to her. "As long as you and I are spending the day together, everything else is a bonus." She tilts her chin up to me, awaiting a kiss. What the lady wants, the lady gets. Dropping a quick kiss on her pretty pink lips, that sweet floral scent of hers does me in. I can't get enough of it.

"Well then, I hope you enjoy, because we're here." I spin her around to see the main gate of the Maltby Street Market.

"A street market?" Her eyes are hidden behind her sunglasses in the afternoon sun, so I can't get a read on her.

"I know it might seem simple, but you were so happy that night at the pub. I figure you'd enjoy something like this. Wandering around, eating and drinking whatever you wanted." Her face wasn't giving anything away. Shite, I completely blew this. "Christ, now this sounds totally lame, and you were probably wanting something—"

She cuts me off by throwing her arms around my neck and planting a long, hard kiss on my lips. My arms hold her close to me as she deepens the kiss for just a moment.

"Sean. This is absolutely perfect. Just spending the day together. It's bloody brilliant. Any day with you is." Her blue eyes are sparkling with excitement as she moves one hand over my cheek. I don't think anyone has ever looked so happy to go to a street market.

"Well then, let's go. I hate to keep the market waiting." She is beside herself with excitement as she grabs my hand and pulls me ahead.

"Ooh, cocktails! Let's get one as we wander around."

Her smile as she turns back to me hits me square in the chest. I don't know where Kat came from or much about her past, but fecking hell, if I'm not falling in love with this pink-haired goddess of a woman.

"Afternoon, there. What'll ya have?" Kat orders both of us a smoked gin and tonic without second thought. She passes over a few pounds, and the bartender hands Kat the two elaborate drinks.

"Cheers, mate." He nods at us as we make our way over to a high-top table.

"This is so good," Kat moans, her eyes closed as she takes a large drink. I lean down and pull her lips into mine. The gin cuts through her sweet taste, but damn, if this kiss isn't delicious.

"Tastes pretty great to me, love." I wink at her as a blush creeps over her pretty face. Whatever is in this drink is bloody amazing.

"I am so glad you decided to bring us here." She cuddles up into my side as we watch people come and go into the market.

"Well, if you enjoy this, there's a great wide world of markets out there for you." The joy coming off of her is palpable. The idea came to me this morning while I was watching her sleep. She was too beautiful to wake up.

Kat rests her hand on my chest, her face relaxed and happy. "As long as you are my guide, I will follow you anywhere."

"I like the sound of that."

"Plus, I get a pretty killer view." She squeezes my arse as she barks out a laugh.

"You had to ruin it with an arse grab." Reaching behind her, I return the favour, pulling her square into me, but I let my hand linger there. The feel of Kat in my arms is unlike anything else. I've never been around a woman who affected me this badly. Just the sound of her voice while we're working makes me happy. It makes me want to plan a million little things like this to keep that smile on her face.

"Sorry, it's a nice arse. I'm pretty sure you didn't mind it last night."

"You might not want to bring that up right now. It would be rather inappropriate for me to be sporting a semi walking around the market." I know she feels it because she's now biting on that blessed bottom lip I want to suck into my mouth.

"Just slightly inappropriate. Now, let's finish these cocktails because I see some baked goods that are calling my name."

Kat slams back her drink, grinning at me as she puts her glass back on the table. She was timid when she first came to the shop, but now, her happiness is contagious. I can't imagine her not being in the shop every day. She puts everyone at ease when they walk in, whether it's their first tattoo or their fiftieth.

I don't know how Kat is feeling, but I'd love to make this thing between us more permanent. She's tight-lipped about where she came from, giving me no details. I don't know if she's running from something, or Christ, someone, but I want her to be a set fixture in my life. Hell, my parents would love her. Pierce loves her. She's so easy to love.

"Sean, which do you want?" I point at the first thing I see, still lost in my thoughts. I can't seem to keep my hands off of her as she waits for the spoils of her hunt. Wrapping my arms around her waist, I pull her back into me. She looks up at me, pulling me further under her spell.

"Hi, love." My voice is barely above a whisper.

"Hello." Her hand grazes my arm, tracing the outlines

of the tattoos there. It's a habit I've noticed, and I don't think she even realises she's doing it. Whether we're lying in bed or eating next to one another, she absently traces the patterns inked on my skin. And it's fucking amazing.

"Listen, Kat—"

"Here you go, ma'am." The baker hands us the pastries, effectively ending my train of thought. I have no idea how to go about asking Kat if she wants to continue doing what we're doing. I have no idea what the future holds, but all I know is I want her with me. But what if she doesn't want the same thing? What if she's just having fun? Taking a break from wherever she came from? Christ, even thinking of her going back to wherever she came from makes my heart twinge inside my chest. I'm way deeper in this than I thought.

"Sean, you coming?" Kat is twisting out of my arms, ready to go explore the market. She tears off a bite of the pastry, and I grab her wrist and bring it to my mouth.

"Cheeky bastard." She is smiling as she says it. Wrapping my arm around her waist, I bring her in for a kiss. I tease her lips with my tongue and she willingly opens for me. I don't care that we're surrounded by people in the middle of the crammed alley. All I care about is her.

It's not until someone bumps into us that I pull away from her.

"We really need to stop doing that in the middle of crowded streets." Her voice is playful as she gazes up at me.

"Love, I never want to stop doing that. Ever."

"Promise?"

"With every fibre of my being."

Chapter Fifteen

SEAN

"Pierce, I'm heading upstairs. I'm done."

"We still have two hours until close." He's working on someone as I pack up for the night.

"Perks of being the owner. I'm wiped after that last piece. And to be perfectly honest, I miss Kat." For the first time in a long time, I'm not thinking about my failed art programme, or worrying about the shop. The only thing I'm worrying about is getting to Kat.

"Must be nice to be a kept man." He flips me off as I leave the noise of the parlour behind me for the day. The faint sounds of music drift down to me as I head up the stairs.

"Mmm, something smells good in here, love." Kat is a dream, standing in the kitchen, singing softly to some pop song I've never heard. I let her leave work early tonight because I had a client with a large piece on his back and knew I wouldn't want to take any walk-ins after that. There was no point in her waiting downstairs when she could have been relaxing up here.

"Hey, you. You're done sooner than I thought."

Turning to face me, her face is red from the heat of the stove. "I was going to surprise you and have supper ready, but you'll have to wait."

"No one has ever made me supper before." I wrap my arms around her waist, peeking at what she's cooking. "Curry?"

"It's the one thing I'm good at making."

"I can't wait to try it." I drop a kiss on her neck and she tilts her head, giving me better access. "But I'm hungry for something else." It was a busy day, with lots of new walk-ins and designing pieces for new clients. I've gotten used to sneaking away for lunch with Kat. Instead, I ate in the office between clients while finishing off some pre-made designs. It should scare me how much I've gotten used to her being in my life, but fuck, I love it.

"Alright, you. Go sit, and dinner will be ready soon. I'm not wasting this meal because you can't keep it in your pants."

Dropping my head to her shoulder, I could stand here while she cooks and be perfectly content. But she shoos me away. I grab a beer and sit and watch while she cooks. I'm the luckiest bastard in the world, having this pink-haired goddess fall for me.

"How'd it go this afternoon?" Soft wisps of pink hair fall over her shoulder as she turns to look at me.

"Brilliant. Bloody fucking brilliant. He absolutely loved it, and it was hard, but some of my best work." One of my regulars had an old tattoo on his back that he wanted to cover up. Instead of doing something small, he wanted an intricate pattern of a lion erupting out of Trafalgar Square. The level of detail on the background was incredible, and he was ecstatic with how it turned out.

"I'm sure he loved it. But I'm biased because I love everything you do." She gives me a cheeky wink as she turns the heat off and plates our dinner. Passing my plate to me, she grabs a beer and comes to sit next to me, her knees between mine.

"Christ, this is just what I needed tonight." Inhaling deeply, I shovel a large bite in my mouth. Fuck, if that's not the best curry I've ever had. "Damn, Kat. This is delicious."

"Told you I wouldn't waste this meal." She leans over for a quick kiss before devouring hers. "Because I can't make much, but I can make this well," she says around a huge bite.

"I guess you'll need your energy for later then. I've got big plans for you tonight."

"KAT, I'M STUFFED." We moved over to the bed, leaving the dishes for later. She's curled up into my side, both of us content to stay just like this the rest of the night.

"You didn't have to have seconds. Or thirds. It keeps just fine." Her warm hand drifts lazily across my stomach. Her touch lights me up within seconds. I grab her hand, not quite ready for what she wants.

"You're going to have to hold off on that, love. I can't move." I bring her hand up to my lips, kissing each fingertip on her dainty hand. I can feel her shifting next to me until a waterfall of pink hovers over me.

"You better hurry, Sean, because I'm quite ready for you." She drops her lips to mine in an easy kiss. Easily opening to her, I try to take control, but she pushes for domination. For control. And I give it to her.

Grabbing her hips, I pull her on top of me. Food coma be damned. Her hips have a mind of their own, moving over my rock-hard dick. She breaks the kiss and trails her lips down my scruffy jaw to my ear. "I thought you couldn't move," she whispers, nibbling on my earlobe.

Pulling her to me, I flip us over so she's now under me, a smirk lighting up her face.

"Fuck that, Kat." I waste no time pulling her shirt over her head before losing my own. Seeing the ink I marked on her skin makes me feel possessive. I love that I was the first to tattoo her. The first to mark her beautiful skin. Christ, I feel like a caveman that I know her like this. I never want another person's hands inking her sexy as sin body.

I trace the still bright ink. I can't keep my hands off her. "Fuck, I love seeing my work on you, Kat." She guides my head back down to hers, eager to kiss me.

It's a fight for control as Kat tries to flip us again. Her nails digging into my back just forces me to push her deeper into the bed. "Not so fast. You took care of me tonight. Let me take care of you." Her blue eyes are hazy as she throws her arms over her head.

"I'm at your will, Sean."

"Best words I've heard all night."

Leaning down, I shove the cups of her bra down and pull a hard nipple into my mouth. Her moans are the sexiest sounds I've ever heard. Lavishing the most beautiful set of tits with all the attention, I ignore the rolling of her hips.

"More. I need more, Sean." Her eyes are closed as I kiss my way down her stomach. Ever since that first night, she's let me see her. All of her. She's the most beautiful creature I've ever known. Every time with her is better than the last.

Unbuttoning her jeans, I slowly pull them down her legs, taking her thong with them. Her pussy glistens with anticipation as I take in this woman spread out before me like a feast. Pulling her legs apart, I settle my face between them, giving her a long lick that I know drives her wild.

"Yes!" She's up on her elbows now, looking down at me as I delve my tongue inside of her. Her blue eyes are dark as they stay locked on mine. Spreading her lips apart with one hand, I find her clit with the other. Her pussy clenches around my tongue.

"Someone is enjoying themselves." I pull away ever so slightly, biting the inside of her thigh. I lick the sting away before making my way back to my own personal heaven. Her moans are driving me wild. Everything about Kat drives me wild.

"I'm so close. Please don't stop!" she says on a moan, her voice breathy. Inserting a finger into her tight channel, I pull her clit into my mouth. Between my tongue and my fingers, she explodes around me, shouting my name on her release. My name has never sounded so sweet.

When she finally comes down, her body is limp as I stand next to the bed, fully naked now, stroking my dick as I watch the beauty in front of me.

"Are you just going to stand there? I can think of much better things to do."

"I don't mind the view from where I am." I tweak her nipple between my fingers as I roll my hand over the head of my cock, spreading precum down the hard length.

"I have a better view in mind."

"Yeah?"

Kat pushes off the bed, getting on her knees.

"Kat, no. I want—" But the words are lost as her lips close over the head of my cock. Bliss. Her mouth is pure, unadulterated bliss. Those small hands of hers close around the base, working me from both ends. Just as I grab her hair, I hit the back of her throat.

"Fucking hell." Her warm mouth is working me closer

and closer to blowing my load. The tension coiling at the base of my spine needs a release, but I don't want to come down her throat. Fisting my hand tighter in her hair, my dick glistens as I pull her off me. "I'm coming inside you tonight."

She doesn't say a word, just reaches over to the nightstand and grabs a rubber and rolls it on, giving me a squeeze as she releases me. "Get up here." I pull her up into my arms and wrap her legs around my waist, leaning her against the wall. There's no finesse. No easy pace. It's an all-consuming need as I slide easily into her slick pussy.

I bury my face in her neck to try and stave off an instant orgasm. But it's hard. So damn hard when the smell of her surrounds me. When her pussy is clamping down around me. With a subtle move of her hips, I start moving. I set a punishing pace as I bite down on the tender flesh of her skin. Kat's hands are everywhere, clutching me to her as my movements become more hurried.

"Oh, God! I'm coming!" My back is going to be scratched to hell tomorrow, but damn, if it doesn't feel amazing as she shatters around me. She clutches me to her chest as I take a nipple into my mouth and tease her through her own release. I'm close, but I want another orgasm out of my pink-haired goddess.

Pulling out of her, I drop her legs from my waist and turn her to face the wall. "Don't think that's all for you tonight," I whisper in her ear.

"I don't think I can take it." She's breathing heavily, but when I reach around to find her clit again, she leans into my touch.

"You sure about that?" I'm rubbing my dick in the cleft of her ass as she rocks into me.

"Please don't stop."

"Your wish is my command, love." And I don't stop.

My fingers work her clit, driving her crazy. We're chest to back, not a breath of air between us, our skin sweat-slicked from the intensity of our passion. The air crackles around us.

"Sean. I need you inside me. Now." Her hand is on mine, our fingers now working her as I easily slide home into her pussy, chasing my own release. Fire speeds down my spine as Kat comes again, pulling my orgasm out of me. Fuck, if I'm not having the best sex of my life with Kat.

Kat is limp beneath me, completely sated. Moving my hand up to her stomach, I hold her up against me. I'm not ready to leave her warmth. There's something about this woman that settles me. That quiets the voice of failure in my head that I couldn't make my art programme work.

"Sean. I need to lie down. I don't know how much longer I can stand. You've turned me into jelly." Pride surges through me.

Using my weight to keep her up, I pull out and tie off the rubber. Pulling her into my arms, I carry her over to the bed and lie down next to her, keeping her close to my side. I'm absolutely spent, and the feel of her breathing at my side lulls me to sleep, but not before I hear her whispered words, "How in the world am I going to keep you, Sean?"

Chapter Sixteen

KAT

"Shite. That's all wrong." Sean's annoyed voice carries through the store. He's been on edge all day for some reason, and I can't pinpoint why. His brow is furrowed in annoyance as he continues working on the design in front of him.

"What's bothering you?" I wrap my arms around his shoulder, trying to stifle his annoyance.

"It's nothing." Well, if that isn't a lie.

"Something is bothering you. Just tell me so I can help."

He puffs out a breath, dropping the pen in his hand. "I can't get this design right, and it bothers me. I'm supposed to have it done by now, and I don't."

I can feel the tension coursing through him. "Why don't you take a break?"

"Because I can't. He's going to be here tomorrow, and I need to have this done." He rips the page out of the notebook, and throws it in the trash. I can only squeeze my arms tighter around him. Sean is a level-headed person, never one to get overly emotional. But right now, he's wound so tight. Tighter than I've seen him these last few weeks.

"Let's get out of here. We can come back later and work on this."

"I need to get it done tonight, Kat." His voice is short, something I've never heard from him before. It further strengthens my resolve.

"You need a break. Let's get out of here for dinner."

"I need to finish."

I grab the notebook from the desk and pull it out of his reach. I've never seen Sean so wrapped up in a design before. I admire his dedication to his job, but it isn't going to help anyone when he is wound so tight.

"Let's go."

"Go where?" he asks.

"Somewhere that's not here. You need a break." As I smooth my hands over his hair, he finally looks like he is relaxing. His face is contemplative as he looks at me.

"Can I show you something?" he asks.

"Anything." Sean stands up as he pulls me into an embrace. There is no place I'd rather be than there in his arms.

"Boys, watch the shop. I'll be back later."

He doesn't wait for an answer. Sean laces his fingers through my hands as he pulls me out the door.

———

"SEAN, WHERE ARE WE GOING?" We've been walking for an interminable time, with no end in sight.

"You really don't like surprises, do you?" His arm is around my shoulders as he pulls me to a stop. "Here we are." We're standing in front of an old brick building with brown paper covering the windows. "I know it's not much to look at, but let me show you."

"This place is yours?" Sean holds the door open as I walk inside. My eyes are immediately drawn to strands of lights hanging from the ceiling. Desks are lined up with a few chairs, but not much else.

"What is this place?"

Sean's hands are tucked into his pockets, as he shyly looks around the space. "This is what has been taking up so much of my time these last few months. I've been trying to get an art programme off the ground."

"An art programme?" My head is spinning as I try to piece together what he is saying.

"Mum worked when we were little, so Pierce and I always had to have somewhere to go after school. It wasn't until we found a small art school that I realized what I wanted to do with my life. There's nothing like it around here, so I wanted to start my own programme for kids in this area."

His voice is quiet as he takes me in his arms, burying his head in my neck.

"And why isn't it up and running yet?"

His breath is heavy as he lets out a lingering sigh. "I had a few people who were going to back me, but they pulled out at the last minute. I sank all of my savings into leasing this place, and I had nothing left."

I'm at a loss for words when realization strikes like a hammer. The event that Granddad and I were supposed to go to. We were coming here, I know it. My breath leaves in a whoosh. Would Sean and I have been fated to meet? Would we have had the same connection if we met that day as a princess and one of her citizens?

"Sean. This is absolutely brilliant. Is there anything I can do to help?" My mind starts working as I think of who

I could contact to be a donor for such an incredible programme.

"I love that you're willing to help, but I've pulled back on it. I still have the space, but I'm wary of asking for help now."

"Is this why you've been so tense? Why you were so upset about losing that job?"

He nods his head. "I thought I did a pretty good job hiding it. I just feel like such a failure because I couldn't make it work."

"No." My voice is hard. I want him to know that he is anything but a failure. He could never be a failure in my eyes. "It's just delayed."

I turn in his arms and cup his cheeks, my fingers dancing over his lips. I was in deep before with him, but hearing what he wants to do? I've fallen even harder for this man. This kind, thoughtful, wonderful man. It should scare me at how quickly I'm developing these feelings for him, but it doesn't.

"I love your confidence in me, Kat." Sean's eyes are soft as they skim over my face.

"Whatever help you need, I'm here." I brush my lips over his as my fingers tangle in the soft strands at the nape of his neck. If there's one thing I can do, it's help Sean get this programme started. I have no idea what is going to happen in my life in these next few weeks, but I know I can help him with this wherever I end up.

"Okay, enough depressing talk." He tries to laugh it off and walks across the room to peer out a window, but I can see just how upset he is that this stalled. It makes my chest ache that he wasn't able to get this started.

Not one single person I've dated would have ever thought to do something like this. The men I have dated— if you want to call them that—only wanted to further their station in life with a princess. But not Sean. No. I have never met a more selfless man. He has the biggest heart.

"Not depressing. This is incredible." My voice is full of awe as I take in the rest of the space around me. I make a vow that no matter what happens, I will make this dream of his a reality. I don't want him to forget about this amazing place even after I leave.

"I'm glad you think so." There's a bitterness to his voice I'm not used to, and it breaks my heart for him.

I walk to him, wrapping my arms around his waist and looking into his sad eyes. His eyes are anything but hopeful. I can see that it's been a long day for him, but I have faith in him.

He cups my cheeks, his deep blue eyes reflecting emotions that I don't want to name. Lust. Desire. Passion. Love. That last one is what scares me most of all. Because how in the world am I supposed to keep this man?

"Where in the world did you come from?" His voice is quiet in the small space as his lips come down on mine. He wants to deepen the kiss, but I don't let him. This place is a sacred space to him, and I don't want it tarnished when I have to leave him.

"Sean." I pull back from him, taking in his soft, sad features. "Make no mistake. Come hell or high water, I will do whatever it takes to make this dream of yours a reality. You deserve this."

"What did I do to deserve you?" His voice is quiet as he gazes at me.

"You took me in. When I needed a place to land, you caught me."

His eyes are heavy with emotion. There is nothing I want more in this world than Sean. He's made it easy to fall for him. "Love, you make it easy to catch you. I'd walk through fire to rescue you from the clutches of the world."

My knees go weak at his words. I've never believed a man's words more than his. It's the hardest fall of my life, but it's also the best one of my life. "I only want to stop falling if it's with you."

"I'm waiting, love. I'm right here, waiting to catch you."

Chapter Seventeen

KAT

"We're getting off early tonight, love. I've got plans for you." Sean's voice is a whisper in my ear. His hot breath sends tingles down my spine. We don't even have to be in the same space and my body lights up just being aware of him. The stolen glances while he's prepping his station, the casual touches when he's passing by me while I'm on the phone. My body seeks him out wherever he is.

After last night, the connection to Sean is even stronger. Sean fell asleep early, but I stayed awake, staring at the man I'm falling in love with. Would we have met if his programme had been funded? Could we still have ended up together?

All I know is, it's getting harder and harder to hide who I really am. My royal holiday is almost up, and I don't want to lose what we have. I don't want to go back to the palace and know Sean is over here and not be able to have him in my life.

"Something you had in mind?" It's been a slower than normal day at the shop without a lot of walk-ins. I like staying busy. It keeps my mind from wondering what will happen when my supposed holiday is over.

"I have a surprise for you tonight." He brushes the long strands of my hair away from my shoulder and drops a kiss on my neck. How I love his lips there.

"I guess I can be pulled away for a few hours." Looking up at him, I watch a smile brighten his face. I can never get my fill of his handsome features. I joke about it quite often, but he really is my own James Bond. This strong, devilishly handsome man who swept me off my feet. He may not be saving the world, but he's certainly changing mine.

"Dress warmly then. Might be a cool evening." Sean pulls my lips into a sweet kiss before heading back to his office. He walks backwards, facing me the entire time, giving me a wink before he goes through the door. A blush creeps up over my neck and face. This man.

I never thought I would meet someone when I decided to break away from my everyday life. I'm feeling things for this man that I've never felt before. That I never thought I would feel for someone. But here I am, falling for the most perfect man I may never get to call my own.

Saved from my own wayward thoughts, I turn my attention back to the woman who just entered the shop. "Excuse me, miss?"

———

"WHERE ARE YOU TAKING ME?" We're strolling along the Thames, the late evening sun casting deep pinks and oranges that give way to purples and blues across the London skyline. It's the perfect evening. There's a bite in the air, but it's not cold enough to stay curled up at home.

"I'm surprised you haven't figured it out yet." Being in the Westminster area of London has my nerves pulling tighter than they have been these last few weeks. Even the mere proximity to the palace has me unnerved. Sean's warm hand laced through mine keeps me here in the moment with him.

"All I see is Big Ben and The Eye. Are we going for a ride?" I pull him in closer to me, resting my chin on his bicep.

"Different kind of ride, love." He points to a dock just before the famous Ferris wheel. A large boat lined with seats and an awning awaits the passengers in line.

I stop, causing people to swerve around us. "A boat ride?"

I can't hide the awe in my voice. I can't believe he remembered that I wanted to do this. I mentioned it in passing at the pub that night. The fact that he didn't chalk it up to my drunken ramblings that night causes tears to blur my vision.

"Are you not happy?" Worry mars his handsome face as he pulls us out of the main walkway.

"Sean, this is…" I can't seem to find the words. Never has anyone done something so thoughtful for me without wanting anything in return. So instead of telling him, I show him. Cupping his face in my hands, I pull him down for a kiss. His hands fist through the pink strands of my hair as he tucks me in close to him. Gently caressing the seam of his lips, he opens to me, my tongue desperately seeking his. Languid, massaging strokes as we stand here in each other's arms surrounded by some of the most recognizable of London's landmarks, the most famous of which starts tolling her famed bells.

"Saved by the bell, I guess." Sean tucks a loose strand of hair behind my ear. His eyes are hazy, staring down at me, and I'm wishing we could continue this kiss, but only in more private quarters.

"C'mon. I don't want to be late." Lacing our hands together again, Sean leads us over to the boat that will guide us through the city tonight.

———

"AND ON YOUR left is the famous Tower of London." Tourists are oohing and ahhing as the famous building comes into sight. Being a royal, I've gone there more times than I can count. But sitting here, on this boat with Sean, pints in our hands, I couldn't be enjoying the view more.

"So, is this everything you hoped it would be?" Sean and I are tucked in the back of the boat, away from the rest of the people. The Tower Bridge looms large ahead of us. Beer lingers on his lips after he takes a long pull.

Reaching up to wipe it away, I give him what can only be described as a million-watt smile. "This is the most wonderful thing anyone has ever done for me." I stay close to him, my face pressed against his neck. The smell of fresh laundry mixes with the cold spring air. It's a simple thing, what Sean did for me. But considering the schedule of my daily life, I never get to see my city like this, as if we're tourists ourselves.

"I would give you many more nights like this. Just say the word." Sean's gaze never wavers from mine. The sights surrounding us blur into the background. It's just the two of us. It makes my heart ache. I want every night to be like this with Sean. I don't care where we are, as long as it's just the two of us.

But I don't know how I can make that happen. Sean is so focused on the shop and his failed programme that I don't know how we could ever begin to make this work in the real world. In the royal world.

As if he can sense my thoughts pulling away from the

now, his voice is a calming reassurance. "Look." One word and he's turning my thoughts to the bridge ahead of us. We're treading water where we are as the bridge starts to rise.

"What a treat we have for you tonight!" The tour guide's excited voice booms over the speakers as everyone rushes to the front of the boat to see the opening of the bridge. Sean and I stay where we are, content in one another's arms. The sting of the wind isn't felt with the warmth swirling between the two of us.

"Legend has it that it's good luck to see the bridge open." The guide drops facts about the bridge as it's raised to allow for the passing of another ship.

"I'll take all the luck I can get." I can feel his lips at my temple. My pulse starts racing as I take in the meaning of his words. It can't mean what I think it means, can it? I start to turn, but Sean keeps his arm firmly around my shoulders.

"I love you, Kat." There's a tug in my chest when he says my name. Not my real name, but one of my names nevertheless. "I don't know where you came from, or where you're going, but I have fallen hopelessly in love with you."

This time, when I go to face him, he doesn't stop me. Setting my drink down, I wrap my arms around him and bury my face in his neck. The words spill from my lips before I have a hope of stopping them. "I love you, Sean." There's more I want to say, but I can't. What is there to say? Come back with me to the palace? Give up your entire life and watch me get torn to bits by the media?

Instead, I squeeze him to me as he pulls me into his lap. No one is paying us any attention. We're still stationary in the water as the larger vessel drifts slowly by us. No more words are said as we stay like this. This is the only place I want to be.

The gunning of the boat engine breaks our moment. Sean's smile is soft as my fingers drift lazily over the stubble on his jaw. He catches my hand and brings it over his heart. The beat is rapid, matching my own. No doubt he can feel it where his fingers graze my wrist.

My heart continues to beat quickly as a feeling of loss takes over. I can't explain it, but in this moment, I feel like I'm losing Sean. There's still time before I have to be back at the palace. But how do I go about explaining to this man who I really am? Will he be able to move past the fact that I'm a princess, never mind that I've been lying to him these last few weeks?

Tomorrow. I'll tell Sean tomorrow. I don't know what is going to happen, but I can't lose this man. He's too important to me.

"Let's go home. Make love to me, Sean." My voice comes out broken, filled with lust and a sense of overwhelming urgency.

"There is nothing I want more in the world."

Chapter Eighteen

SEAN

Kat's mood has been up and down all night. I don't know what is going on with her, but she seems happy again. It's almost as if my confession of loving her threw her for a loop. I couldn't contain the words as they spilled out. But as soon as I said them, I knew it was right. I don't know what is going to happen with the two of us, but right now it doesn't matter. Because only Kat matters. And loving my pink-haired goddess of a woman.

We leave the boat tour quickly. I had planned to go for dinner and drinks, but we just need to be with one another. Because as soon as we make it back to the studio, clothes are shed as we race up the stairs. She wastes no time unclasping her bra and dropping it at my feet.

"Fuck, Kat. You are fecking gorgeous. The things I want to do to you." My voice is a growl as I lean down to take a pert nipple into my mouth. Her hands in my hair guide my motions. I know she's enjoying it when her grip tightens, causing the slightest bit of pain to turn into pleasure. I'm hard as a rock, my zipper no doubt carving permanent marks into my dick.

Grabbing Kat around the waist, I carry her to our bed. This used to be a place I crashed when I stayed too late at the shop. It's crazy how quickly I've come to think of it as our place. Letting this stranger stay here turned out to be one of the best things I've ever done.

Laying her in the center of the bed, I pull back and can't help but cast my gaze over her. Kneeling between her legs, my fingers ghost up and down her sides. Goose pimples break out in my trail. Placing my hands on each side of her head, I lean over her, locking those blue eyes with mine. Words aren't said, but emotion is heavy in the air.

Sure, I've had my fair share of women before, but never love. Never like this. "Fuck, Kat. I love you." Her hands join around my neck and pull me down to her, our lips crashing together in a want I've never felt. It's almost like she's memorizing my lips and the lingering taste of our earlier drinks. The touch, the feel of my lips against hers makes her cry out in delight. I kiss a trail along her jaw to the spot on her neck that she loves so much.

I suck down hard, then lick the sting away. I don't think I've given someone a hickey since high school, but there's an overwhelming sense to mark her as mine. To let other men know they need to back off. The rocking of her hips against mine tells me she liked it. So I do it again, this time moving lower.

"God, Sean. That feels so damn good." Her nails cut into my back, pulling me in closer to her. Her nipples are hard against my chest as her powerful thighs squeeze around my waist.

I move down her chest, kissing and sucking as I go. She is a writhing mess beneath me as I kiss my way over her soft stomach. I've learned the feel of each and every one of her curves these last few weeks and I cannot get enough of them.

Pulling her legs off of me, I slowly undo her jeans. More slowly than I usually do, because I love to drive her wild. I kiss just above her thong as I pull them down her legs, not quite relieving her of her need.

"Stop teasing me!" she shouts. Kat's hands are in her hair, desperate need wafting off of her.

"Just for that, I think I'll take my time." I kiss her through the lace fabric, loving the smell of her need. I palm my dick through my jeans to keep my own pleasure at bay. It's not important right now. Right now, making Kat feel incredible is the only thing in the world that matters.

Running a finger slowly over the wet fabric, I grin down at her. She's biting down on her bottom lip, head thrown back in pleasure. "Seems like you need some relief." Playfulness laces my voice. I love worshipping every bit of this woman, but seeing her outright frustration at her need for me is the best kind of turn-on.

"Please, Sean. Please, please, please." She is muttering incoherent words as I slide my finger beneath the small swath of fabric, not bothering to move it. Just as I can see she's about to yell at me again, I dive two fingers into her tight channel. Her back bows off the bed as I start pumping my fingers in and out of her. The time for games is over.

Bending over, I rip the fabric away from her body as I take her clit in my mouth. "Mmm, that feels so damn good." Her fingers pull my hair taut as she guides my movements. A smile plays at my lips while my tongue works. Even when I'm in control, she has all the power. I would move heaven and earth to make this woman happy in the smallest of ways.

Kat is close. Her pussy is clenching around my fingers

as I continue driving into her. The breathy sounds she makes get louder the closer she gets.

"Sean. Sean, oh yes! Oh God, yes!" She spasms around me as she comes. She rocks into my mouth as she rides out her orgasm, those thighs I love so much squeezing tight around my head.

As she comes down, I pull back, releasing my dick from his denim prison. Kat's a blissed-out goddess, laid out like a feast before a god returning from battle.

Pushing herself up, she gets down before me on her knees. And when she draws my cock into her hot mouth? I feel like a god. She takes me as far as she can, her other hand working my balls over. Those delicate, feminine fingers know just how to drive me into a frenzy.

Lightning pleasure courses through my body, settling at the base of my back. My balls get tighter as she continues laving me with attention. I'll never get enough of her mouth on me. This perfect goddess of a woman is my dream. Nothing else matters but her. And as much as I would love to come in that pretty mouth of hers, I don't want to. I want to be balls deep in my woman when I explode.

Grabbing her by the chin, I pull out of her mouth, a small trail of saliva creating a tiny thread between us. Wiping her swollen lips clean, I lift her back up onto the bed. Being the cheeky woman she is, she gets on all fours, shaking her ass at me. I can't resist. Grabbing a rubber, I roll it over my hard length as I sink my teeth into her luscious arse.

"You ready for me, love?" I rub the head of my dick through her crack, to her wet pussy.

"Always."

I waste no time, driving balls deep into her. I have to think of everything I do to prep my station so I don't come too early. Being inside of Kat is a heaven I've never experienced before I met her. I never want to forget this feeling.

Once I'm sure I won't lose it, I set a punishing pace. Her body responds to every touch as my hands caress the expanse of her back. They glide over the intricate lines now inked on her side. Her once virgin skin that is now permanently altered at my hand.

"Fuck, Kat." My thrusts are driving her farther up the bed, her head now pushed into the sheets, as she holds on for dear life. An epic orgasm is building. Leaning over her, I use the wall for leverage, rolling my hips every time I hit that sweet spot inside of her.

"Oh God, I'm coming!" Her voice is muffled as I feel her clenching around me. It would be enough to draw an orgasm from a lesser mortal. But I want another orgasm out of her before I come. Her pleasure is the only thing that matters right now.

Not letting her catch her breath, I cover her back with my chest. Moving one hand down, I grab her hand and tangle it with mine, bringing it to her clit. I slow my punishing pace ever so slightly as our fingers dance over her clit.

Kat's head turns underneath me, flushed pink from her orgasm. "Kiss me."

Her head turns to capture my lips as we both move closer and closer to release. Our lips barely touch as our hot breaths mingle.

"Sean, I'm almost there. Please don't stop. Don't ever stop." I capture her pleas with my lips as her hand moves in a frenzied pace on her clit. I remove my hand and grip her hips, resuming the pace I set earlier. I'm gripping so tight, it'll leave bruises, but that only heightens my need for her.

As she starts to come, I can feel myself ready for

release. Pulling out of her, I rip the rubber off and work my dick as thick spurts of cum paint her back. My head is thrown back in pleasure and I can't keep the groan inside at the picture before me. I haven't seen anything so sexy in my life.

My body is spent after the best orgasm of my life. I know I should clean us up, but I collapse next to Kat on the bed. Her beautiful blue eyes are staring at me with nothing but love. Tucking a pink strand of hair behind her ear, I grab my boxers from the end of the bed to wipe her off. She doesn't move. Her arms are tucked under her chin as her eyes drift shut.

"Sean?" I spoon into her side, not wanting an ounce of air between us.

"Kat?"

"Promise we'll never stop doing that?" I'm losing her to sleep, so I can only whisper to her as sleep pulls me under.

"Every day, love. I'll worship you every day."

———

THE PIERCING SOUND of the phone cuts through my sleep. Who the fuck is calling me this late? The clock shows three in the morning. Bloody hell. It's quiet again before the shrill piercing cuts in again. Reaching for the nightstand next to me, I grab the phone and answer quietly, trying not to wake Kat. Her chest rises and falls with her soft breaths. The sheet has slipped low, exposing her sexy tits.

"Hello?" My voice is scratchy when I answer.

"Who the fuck is this?" the voice on the other end shouts.

"You're calling me. You tell me." Nothing like being awakened to a wrong number in the middle of the night.

"What are you doing with Ellie's phone?" My brain is tired. Exhausted from making love to Kat all night. I'm not in the mood to dick around with this guy.

"You've got the wrong number, buddy. No Ellie here." I go to hang up, but a soft hand on my bicep pulls me away. Kat's face is strained.

"Give me the phone, Sean." Confused, I hand her the phone, seeing the name on the screen. Jamie. Who the bloody hell is Jamie?

"Jamie? Why are you calling so late?" The voice on the other end is muffled, but the colour drains from Kat's face. Standing, I grab the sweats next to the bed and quickly pull them on. Her hand covers her face, tears now glistening in her eyes.

"It can't be true, Jamie. It can't be." I can only look on in confusion. Who is this Ellie person, and why does Kat have her phone?

My confusion only grows as she mutters her next words, "God Save the King."

Chapter Nineteen

ELLIE

Pulling the sheet up over my bare chest, I look Sean in the eye. Confusion mars his beautiful features. Pain laces my heart that this might be one of the last times I see him. I was supposed to tell him tomorrow. He wasn't supposed to find out like this.

Jamie's words echo in my head. The king had a stroke and isn't expected to make it to morning. I need to come back to the palace now. I have to leave behind this life that I have no right to.

"I'll call my PPOs and get to the palace as soon as I can. Are you there now?" I'm staring into Sean's eyes. The confusion gives way to anger as I can see him looking more closely at me, studying my features in a way he never did before. I shake my head, hoping to tell him I'll explain everything as soon as I end this call. This life-changing call I never wanted to receive.

"They are there now. Do you really think I wouldn't have found you and kept you safe on this little adventure?" His voice is sharp, hard. So unlike my playful brother.

"What in the world are you talking about?" Hurt laces my tone.

"You really think the heir to the throne could go off and fuck around with some tattoo artist and we wouldn't have eyes on you?" The hurtful words stun me.

"Fuck off, James. I'll see you when I see you." I end the call and throw the phone down on the bed. Pressing the heels of my hands into my eyes, I need to keep it together. My sweet granddad is going to die. The lively man who used to sled with us during the holidays. Who would tell us the sordid history of our family when no one else would. The strongest leader our country has ever seen.

"Kat. What in the world is going on?" Sean's voice is quiet. This can't be it. This can't be the end with the only man I've loved. "Or is Kat even your name?"

I wince. Of course he would have heard Jamie calling me Ellie. "Kat is my middle name."

"And why is it you go by your middle name?" He starts pacing, an anxious energy rippling off of him.

"Because I didn't want you to know who I really was."

The look he gives me could cut glass. The pain I feel will be nothing when I deliver this blow. Worse than a sword penetrating armour.

"Because you have a husband at home? Wanted to play around?"

I stand, the sheet falling away from me. Looking for my bag and clothes, I have to start packing up what little I have here. Sweeping it all away like this piece of me never existed.

"Because my real name is Eleanor. Princess Eleanor Katherine Jane."

Sean stares back at me as if he's never met me. I sweep by him, trying to quickly dress when he grabs my arm and pulls me back to him. My still naked chest hits his bare one. My hand lands on his pec and the tattoos there that have become so familiar to me.

"What the hell do you mean, princess?" His voice is acid. I look down, our toes touching. My breath hitches, pain and sadness threatening to pull me under.

"Just what I said. I'm second in line to the throne. Technically, first now." I wince at that thought.

"First?"

"That was my brother on the phone. Jamie, or Prince James as you know him. My grandfather, the king, had a stroke. He isn't expected to make it through the night. I have to go home. Now."

I take advantage of his stunned silence to break free of his hold. Grabbing the first clothes I can find, I dress quickly and throw everything else in my bag.

"So what the fuck has this been these last few weeks then? Just some game to you?" Only years of training for dealing with the press and public events keeps my features even. The hurt in his voice is devastating.

"Of course it wasn't, Sean. I know this sounds terrible to say, but I hate my life in the palace. The overbearing eyes that watch what I do at all times of the day. The tabloids monitoring how I look and what I wear. The stuffiness. All I want is a quiet life, so I ran. And I ran into you."

He shakes his head, going back to the pacing. I step into my shoes, knowing the PPOs will be up here in the next five minutes if I'm not in the waiting car, speeding back to the palace.

"How lucky for me then." He's muttering to himself as I watch him. My bag slung is over my shoulder, but I don't want to leave him like this.

"Please, Sean. I just wanted time away from my life. From the structure and never-ending events. It's not me. I hate it. All I want is to have my own flat and a job I love. I was going to tell you tomorrow."

"You were going to tell me? Easy to say now that the secret is out."

One bloody phone call ripped away any chance for a future the two of us might have had. If only I could have explained it to him myself. If only Jamie didn't have to call with the worst news imaginable. This wasn't supposed to happen.

"Sean. Please, I can't explain right now. Just, believe me. Believe me that this was real. That everything I feel for you is real." Shite, there isn't enough time. "I have to—" The loud banging on the stairs pulls our attention to the door, seconds before my PPOs burst in.

"And I guess now we'll never know." He sits on the bed, his back to me. The air in the room is rife with nervous energy—mine at having to leave Sean and my PPOs at getting me back to the palace. But I can't leave him like this. He has to know that everything I felt for him was real. You can't fake those kinds of emotions.

I wrap my hand around his neck, dropping my head to his.

"I love you, Sean. And no matter what you think, this wasn't a game. It was real for me. And I will *always* love you." I kiss his head and walk towards my security officers.

————

THE MOOD at the palace is somber. Staff loiter around the halls. Rumours are undoubtedly being passed as to what is happening. The security detail takes me straight to the private quarters. Looks and whispers linger in my wake at my disheveled appearance. I ignore them all. The only person I want to see may not even realize I am there.

"Ellie!" A familiar voice bellows behind me. Jamie comes running up to me, in his own state of disarray. He slows to a stop in front of me, taking in my appearance. "What did you do to yourself?" He plays with a piece of my pink hair. I stare down, now realizing I'm standing in joggers and Sean's old grey shirt I loved so much. His familiar scent is the only thing keeping me grounded right now. Even though he probably hates me. I'll never forget the look on his face when he found out who I am.

"Had to make myself harder to recognize." I glance up into his red-rimmed eyes. "We can talk about it later. I want to see Granddad."

"You're in no state to see him right now."

"Well, I really don't give a shite what you think. I'd rather see him like this than be presentable and not have the chance. So shove off, James." He rears back. I knew the blow would land the second I used his full name. In a right fit, I stomp off towards my granddad's bedroom where his own security officers stand guard outside.

"May I see him, please?" They give me a once-over, before nodding and opening the door.

The beep of the heart rate monitor is the only thing heard in the large room. The soft glow of lamps creates an ominous mood. My grandmum is sitting in a chair at my granddad's bedside. My mum and dad stand behind her with my aunt and uncle. I move farther into the room, my presence still not known until Jamie comes up beside me, clearing his throat. All eyes turn to him. Then me. I can feel the reproachful glares.

"Eleanor. What have you done with yourself?" My mother's voice is full of consternation. The pink hair must be a shock. I can only imagine what they would think if they saw the tattoo underneath. I move closer to my grand-dad's bed. The once formidable king is small, already starting to fade away. I set my hand down on my grand-mum's shoulder, giving it a brief squeeze. Her wrinkly hand clutches mine. Her glassy eyes turn to me.

"You were always your grandfather's favourite." Her voice is solemn. Quiet. "Take a moment with him." She stands, giving me a peck on the cheek as she ushers everyone out to the sitting room. As the door closes, the dam on my emotions starts to break. Tears well in my eyes. All the emotion from the last hour is simmering, waiting to break free. I go to sit on the edge of the bed and take his still warm hand in mine, giving it a brief squeeze.

"I'm sorry I wasn't here, Granddad. But I hope you know how much I love you. Now that Mum is taking over, I really don't know what to do." I look down at our clasped hands. The ring of our family crest sits loose on his thin finger.

"These last few weeks with Sean have been the best of my life. I wish you could have met him. You would've liked him. Kind. Caring. Funny. Everything I've always wanted. I know I was born into this, but you know it's never what I wanted. A quiet, simple life. The kind of love you and Grandmum had. But I think I've lost it. I wish you could tell me what to do, but it's not possible. I'm going to miss you and your guidance so much. I love you." I kiss the back of his hand, not wanting him to leave this world.

It gets harder to breathe the farther away from him I get. The only person I want right now hates me. Leaving Granddad's room behind, I'm adrift. I don't know where to go when a steadying hand comes down on my shoulder.

"Come, my darling. Let's get you straightened out." My mum's voice is clear. I hate that my granddad will be gone from this world in a few hours' time. My mom's arm wraps around my waist, guiding me towards her room. Her stylists are there, ready to fix me up.

"We'll talk about this later." She waves her hand over my appearance. "But right now, we have other things to tend to. James will be waiting outside for you once you're finished. I'm going back to sit with Mum."

"I don't need a babysitter." My voice is scratchy and harsher than I intended it to be.

"That remains to be seen, young lady. Now, we'll get you taken care of and get you appropriate attire for what will no doubt be a terrible moment. I'm sorry you had to come home like this."

She is out of the room, and the stylists descend on me. Before they start yanking my clothes off, I grab the robe that's being held in front of me.

"Stop. Please. Just let me have a moment."

Heading into the loo, I take stock of my appearance. My eyes are dull and my cheeks sunken as I strip out of Sean's shirt and cover myself up with the robe. The lingering smell is the final straw. Tears rush from my eyes as the dam finally breaks and the overwhelming emotions crash into me. The loss of my granddad, the larger-than-life man who has always been in my life and the loss of Sean, my new love, and the life that could have been.

"Your Highness." Alice is at my side, squeezing me into her. "Everything will be alright." Her voice is oddly comforting as my heart is breaking.

With not even a moment to reflect, I'm being pulled out of the loo. The stylists are attacking my pink hair. I don't pay attention to the whispers around me as I'm plucked and prodded to within a centimetre of my life. I close my eyes, blocking out the world around me and wishing with every fibre of my being that I could take back these last few hours.

Chapter Twenty

ELLIE

Breaking News

British News Network is reporting that King Edward has suffered a stroke and passed away early this morning. The Queen, his two children, and their families were by his side. Princess Katherine will now be the reigning monarch of our beloved nation. More to come on this developing story.

The last few hours have been a whirlwind of the worst kind, blending from one after the other into the next. The whole family was here as our beloved granddad slowly slipped away. We were given a few short hours before we had to make ourselves presentable.

I'm in a simple black cape dress, with my hair now restored to its natural colour and pulled back into a low bun. Our pictures are being snapped as we leave the palace. Crowds are gathering at the gates and calling for our attention. A sea of flowers stretches as far as the eye can see.

My face is devoid of any emotion as Jamie and I slip into the car to take us back to Clarence House with the rest of the family. I'm trying to keep it together as best I can. My heart shattered hours ago, and I'm not sure if it will ever be fully put back together. The death of my beloved grandfather. The loss of Sean. My future changed before my eyes, as I'm now the first in line for the throne.

"Are you going to speak to me? Or are you going to wallow all day over there?" Jamie's voice is cold. Staring out the dark tinted windows, I don't bother with looking at him. Anger is firing through my body at his earlier words, still ringing in my head.

"No, I don't think I will." We drive through a wall of noise as we leave the palace to make our way to Mum's. It's then a paralyzing thought hits me. It will no longer be Mum's house. It's the residence of the heir apparent. A sickness washes over me at the thought.

"You look like you're going to be sick. Are you okay?" Jamie's hand comes down on my arm as I try to take in deep breaths.

"No, I'm not okay, you daft idiot!" I shove his hand off of me, as my voice carries in the small space. All eyes are on me. "The world is changing before our eyes, and you have the audacity to ask me if I'm okay!"

"You need to pull it together, Ellie." His voice is harsh this time.

"Don't you think I know that?" I hiss. I don't have the luxury of losing it in public. While the nation gets to mourn their king, we have to hide our grief. Keep calm and carry on. "Now, in the interest of 'pulling it together,' leave me be."

The short drive to Clarence House feels endless. The

crowds around the palace are enormous and growing by the minute. Mum and Dad are waiting for us with Uncle Albert and Aunt Helena. Grandmum is still at the palace. There are protocols in place when the king or queen dies. But right now, everyone looks out of sorts.

"Ellie. Come with me." Charlotte is at my side, pulling me into the house. Leading me to a small sitting room upstairs, she keeps her hands in mine.

"What has been going on? Where have you been? And why did you show up to the palace with pink hair?" She's firing off questions faster than I can think. My emotions, on a hair trigger now, explode out of me on a sob.

"Oh, darling." She wraps her arms around me as I let the tears flow. I cling to her for dear life, as her hands move over me in a soothing manner.

"Charlotte. I don't know what to do." My voice is shaky. I've lost one of the most important people in my life and will likely never see the other again.

"Ellie. Talk to me. What happened?" Wiping the tears from my face, I tell her everything. From heeding her advice to meeting Sean along the way.

"I fell in love, Charlotte. I love him and I have no idea what to do."

She wipes away the tears still streaking down my face. "Can you talk to him? See how he feels?"

"I lied to him, Charlotte!" I move away from her and start pacing the room. "He was devastated. How will he ever get past that?"

"Eleanor. You need to take a breath. You aren't going to do anyone any good by having a nervous breakdown."

I turn and face her, pinning her with an unwavering gaze. "Have you ever thought that maybe I'm tired of living for everyone else? For once in my life, I was living for myself. And it was incredible. No one was telling me where to be or what to do. And the press wasn't watching my every move. I've never felt more like myself, Charlotte. It was incredible."

"Was it because of Sean?"

The sound of his name causes pain to flash through me. "Yes. No. I made the decision to run away, but meeting him? It gave me a confidence I never knew I had."

"Maybe he feels the same way. Maybe he'll want to stay with you too."

I look around the grand sitting room we're in. It's one of the less formal sitting rooms, yet still older than most of London. "Why would anyone want to take on this world? Sean has his own life. He's building something wonderful that he wouldn't be able to leave."

"Ellie." She walks over to me and wraps me in a hug. I push her away, unable to take her sympathy.

"No. I—" Having kept a lid on my emotions my entire life, it's hard to tamp them back down. "I'm sorry, Charlotte. But I can't discuss this anymore. I have to go."

Rushing out of the sitting room, I follow the hallway to my own room. It's nothing like the small studio apartment I've been staying in for the last few weeks. The entire apartment could fit in my bedroom alone. It's cold and too glamourous for what I need.

All I want, *all I need*, is to feel Sean's arms around me. There's an emptiness in my chest that feels endless. Falling to the bed, I let the tears continue, hoping sleep will eventually take me.

———

"ELEANOR. ARE YOU READY?" Mum's voice is calm. She's been nothing but a beacon of hope in the last week since being proclaimed the reigning monarch. Granddad has been moved to lie in state at Westminster before his service at the end of the week. Mum insisted on one final, private family viewing before the public visitation.

"As I'll ever be."

"My sweet girl. I'm worried about you." I wish her voice had the same calming effect from when I was young, but I'm stuck in my own head.

"There's not much to do about it now. Just need to make it through these next few days, and I'll be okay."

"Will you, though? Every time I look at you, your pain just gets worse and worse. It breaks my heart."

"I'm sorry. I'll try to pull myself together." Easier said than done.

She shakes her head before pulling me in for a hug. "No stiff upper lip with me today, Eleanor. It's going to be a hard day. You're allowed to feel your feelings. I'll be by your side today."

"Mum. That's impossible. You're the queen now." I let out a shaky laugh, the first time in days.

"Bollocks. I'm the queen. If I want to be by my daughter's side today, I will be by her side."

A smile breaks through. A rarity these last few days. I can't imagine the pressure she is under right now. No one wants to become king or queen when it's at the sacrifice of another life.

"Let's go get this day over with." I grab her hand and give it a squeeze. The days have been endless as we get closer to the funeral. It's a day I never want to experience, but it is a part of life.

I only wish I had more time with my grandfather. It never feels like enough time. There is so much wisdom I still could have learned from him. But now, life is looking clearer than ever before. The last few weeks with Sean proved how I am not cut out for this royal life. For being in the spotlight and having my every move watched. Having my every day planned down to the minute.

It took running away for me to realize what I truly want out of life. I want to be able to wake up, go to a job I enjoy, and come home to the person I love. It's simple. It's easy. And there's no easy way to go about getting it. The royal family is in a state of distress, and I don't know how I can further add to it.

Stirring myself away from my thoughts, I follow Mum to the cars that will take us to Westminster. The closer we get to the abbey, the more distraught I become. For the first time in my life, I'm not keeping my emotions in check. As mum said, no stiff upper lip today. People and press line the roads as we make the short drive from the palace. Flowers are flung onto the road as we pass. It only adds to the heaviness of my own emotions today.

There's already a line of people waiting to start the visitation. In all my years of being a royal, I've never felt so on display before. All I want is to go back to that studio apartment and stay curled up until these days are over. But I'm not granted that ability.

Charlotte appears at my side and we walk in behind our parents. The smoky smell of incense lingers through the abbey as we make the long walk to where the king is lying in state. My chest constricts the closer we get to him. And when we finally arrive? I'm inconsolable.

One of the most important people in my life is gone and there is nothing I can do about it. No matter how I try to comfort myself or tell myself it will be better, I'm at an utter loss. Furiously wiping the tears from my face, I try to pull myself together. Jamie comes to my other side, offering me support that I would have rejected any other day. I'm too tired to rebuff him today.

"I'm here, Ellie. It'll be okay. I promise." I can only nod

at his words. His strong arm around my shoulders gives me the strength I need to soldier on through the day. Grandmum is here and the epitome of grace and strength. Not a tear falls from her stoic face as she says her goodbyes to the man she loves. Eighty is too young for a larger-than-life personality to be gone from this world.

But seeing the love my grandparents shared brings a sense of calm over me. It's as if the heavens have finally opened up and the rains have finally cleared. I've experienced the love they had. They were never an arranged marriage. It was love. And I had that with Sean. And that's what I want. It won't be easy, but for the second time in my life, I'm going to do what I want. The rest of the country be damned.

Chapter Twenty-One

SEAN

The buzz of the tattoo gun is the only thing that cuts through the mindless chatter swirling around the tattoo shop. The vibrations keep me from continuing my spiral. The last few weeks have been endless. The day after Kat left, or Eleanor as I should call her, the news was announced that the king had died. It rocked the entire country.

Me? I could only focus on the images of the king's granddaughter as she stood outside the palace. She was no longer my pink-haired goddess. She was the princess that belonged to the nation. And seeing her there with her dull brown hair, not being able to reach out to her, was a hell I don't wish on my worst enemy.

Her eyes are pure torture. The pain flickering in them is more than I can handle. Everywhere in London is a reminder of her. We were never destined to be together. As upset as I was with her, I could see her struggling. I wanted to wrap her in my arms and not let the world touch her.

But I couldn't. So I buried myself in my work. I can't remember the last time I'd done so many tattoos. I'd been busting my arse so I wouldn't think about Kat. Damn…Eleanor.

Finishing up with the client on my table, I send him on his way. Thankfully, I don't have any more appointments for the day. The rain-soaked London day matches my mood. Pierce side-eyes me as I head back to my office. The bastard won't stop pestering me about my attitude.

Sitting in my office, I distract myself with paperwork. For once, I wasn't thinking about the programme I wanted to start or about making more money for the shop. Eleanor pulled my head out of my arse. She fit so perfectly into my life. Never once did I suspect she was a princess. Sure, she was more proper than most of the women I dated, but she slipped seamlessly into my life.

"What in the bloody hell are you still moping about?" Pierce bursts into my office without invitation.

"I'm fine. I'm just trying to get work done." The stare he gives me tells me he doesn't believe me.

"You've been a sad sack ever since Kat left." I wince when he calls her Kat. "Are you really that upset that you're no longer getting any pussy?"

I'm up and out of my chair before I can even think twice. Slamming him against the wall, anger is firing through my veins. "Don't ever talk about her that way."

"Christ, you really are distraught over losing her. Just go talk to her. Whatever you did can't be that bad."

I shove off of him before I do something I know I'll regret. I thought burying myself in my work would help rid her from my mind, but everywhere I turn, memories of Kat overwhelm me.

"What makes you think I did something?" Pierce really can be a wanker.

"It's usually always the man's fault. Hasn't Dad taught you anything?" He laughs to himself. Our dad always told us that if you ever upset a woman, to apologize. I don't know why, because he could do no wrong in Mum's eyes.

"In this case, it's definitely not my fault. I can't go get her back. It's not that simple."

"Why does it have to be that hard? It's not like she's bloody royalty."

I stop dead in my tracks at his comment. There's no way he knows who she actually is. But shit, did I just give it away? The look on his face tells me I did.

"Fuck, are you serious?" His face is a mix of shock and excitement. "Kat is the princess? What? I mean, how?"

"Hell if I know. Kat didn't exactly hand me her CV when she got here. Fuck, Eleanor!" I push my hands through my hair with more force than necessary. My brain is a fucking mess. Hell, I couldn't even go out back without thinking about our day in the park and fucking in the back. Kat wanted to learn everything about running the shop. Just her presence made everyone here happier. I'm well and truly fucked.

"Are you going to be okay?" Pierce now looks at me with concern.

"I'll be fine."

"Bullshit. There is no way you'll be fine. You were about ready to punch me in the face."

"That's because you were being an arsehole."

"Had I known how you felt about her, I wouldn't have said anything."

I give him a skeptical look. "Oh yeah? And how do I feel about her?"

"You're in love, you wanker. Anyone with eyes can see it."

I couldn't argue with him on that point. I'd gone and fallen irrevocably in love with my pink-haired goddess. And now what the hell was I supposed to do?

"I can't be here anymore. I need to get out of town."

"You going to Mum and Dad's? Mum would be very disappointed if you tell her you fell in love with the princess and didn't realize it."

Shit, he was right. She'd never forgive me if she found out I fell in love with her. Damn her and her love of everything royal. The perfect place hits me.

"You think you can cover me for a few weeks?" A last-minute ticket to the states is more than I want to pay, but I can't be anywhere in London. Hell, anywhere in Europe where the recent changes to the British royal family is front and center news.

"Between Trevor and me, I think we can cover. Where are you going to go?"

"The one place in the world that won't be concerned with the royal family."

———

THE MOUNTAINS in the distance are a familiar sight. It's been too long since I've been to Dixon, Idaho. Walking out of the airport, the familiar voice calling my name tugs my attention to him.

"Hey, Pops." My granddad stands almost a head taller than me.

"Seany. I'm so happy you're here." He pulls me in for a hug. We always came to visit him over the summers growing up, and I never appreciated him as much as I do now.

"Thanks for letting me come on such short notice." He pulls me towards his old, beat-up truck. The same truck that he has had since I was in high school. "Still have ol' Betty?"

"You can't get rid of perfection. Now, you gonna tell me why you're here?"

"Can't I just want to come visit my family?" He gives me the side-eye as he pulls out of the airport. Nothing gets by him. I forgot how much I love coming here. We're immediately in the middle of nowhere as we head towards the ranch.

"If you wanted to come visit, you would've planned ahead. Besides, your mom called me and said she was worried."

Fucking Pierce. Couldn't trust him with anything sometimes. If he told Mum about Kat, I'm going to strangle him the next time I see him.

"It's about a girl."

"It always is. Care to explain?" The sun is sinking below the mountains. It looks like everything is on fire. It doesn't hold a candle to London.

"I fell in love with the wrong woman."

Chapter Twenty-Two

ELLIE

"As for the last item of business. The king has a few letters for each of you." The solicitor hands each of us an envelope. The thick stationery with my grandfather's crest and initials is another painful reminder that he is gone.

"I believe that concludes everything for today. You may reach me at the office should you require anything further." The old man snaps his briefcase shut. He bows to each of us before departing. I stare at my name written in my grandfather's tidy handwriting. Jamie has opened his letter and is frowning. My mum across the table is smiling reading hers. Clutching mine to my chest, I stand. I don't want to read this here. Instead, I leave everyone, finding a footman standing at the doors.

"Please call my PPOs. Tell them I wish to leave the palace immediately." I head towards my room. We've been staying here at the palace with everything going on. It's been somewhat easier being all together. Changing into joggers and a jumper, I throw on my rain jacket and head towards our private entrance, my grandfather's letter in my pocket.

"Your Highness. Where are we going today?" my security officer asks.

"Peter Pan statue. Please." I slide into the car. "No entourage. Just you two, please." She nods, closing the door behind me. It's easier for them to grant these requests when I'm not running around London on my own.

I rest my head against the seat of the car. The rain is quiet as we make our way through the city. The drive is quick, as London is not busy in the early Sunday evening. Hitting the entrance to the park, my security officers walk behind me as I follow the path I've known so well throughout the years. The small bronze statue has always spoken to me. Wanting to remain young. Not wanting to become an adult and step in as the reigning monarch of the United Kingdom.

A tree sits behind the bushes across from the statue. My own protected cove to hide away and just sit. To not be seen. Tilting the umbrella that my PPO gave me, I take the letter from my grandfather out of my pocket and begin to read.

My darling granddaughter,

If you are reading this, then my unfortunate end has come. Hopefully I went out, as our friends across the pond say, guns blazing. But likely, it was old age. And in old age comes wisdom. Wisdom I now wish to impart on you.

Don't be beholden to the path that is laid out before you. My dear, you have so much fire and spirit inside of you, that I would hate to see that squeezed out of you. Sometimes, we are born into a certain lot in life. You were afforded one many only dream of. Yet, you dream of a different kind of life.

I will always cherish my time spent with you. Teaching you what I knew about the throne. You teaching me about things only a little girl would know. And in these precious moments with you, I learned the most valuable lesson. That sometimes, you must set free the thing you love the most in the world.

And so, my darling Eleanor, go. Go live your life as you see fit. Maybe I have completely misjudged you, as an old man may not always be of sound mind, but if you want the throne, then lead with all the fire and passion you possess. But, and I think this old man may be spot on, find the life you want to live. There is no shame in not wanting the life you've been given. There may be some pushback, but tell them this old man said you could. No one can fight with the dead king.

My greatest wish for you is to find someone to walk through this life with you. Your grandmother was the love of my life. I hope you experience this kind of great love in your life. You have so much to offer the world, and I hope you find someone who treats you well and can help you navigate this new chapter in your life.

Do not be sad that I am gone, for I will always be with you. I have cherished our time together and cannot wait to see what you do with your life.

Love,
Your favourite Grandfather

A TEN-POUND NOTE slips out from the envelope. Our own private joke over the years. Tears are now flowing freely, splattering on the letter my grandfather left me, knowing exactly the words I needed to hear. Never did I think my distaste for the life I was born into was shown to those around me. I wipe at the tears. The vise that has been squeezing my heart all these years loosens its hold on me. I carefully fold the letter and tuck it inside my jacket. I let the umbrella fall, letting the raindrops hit my face, mixing with my tears.

"Thought I'd find you here." I open my eyes, seeing Jamie standing in front of me. That same look from earlier furrows his brow. I give him a smile as he sits down on the wet ground next to me.

"So, what are you going to do?" His voice is quiet. So unlike the vibrant brother I'm used to. These last weeks have been strained between us.

"I think if you're asking, you already know." I reach over and take his hand, giving it a squeeze. He lets out a heavy breath.

"Grandfather is quite sneaky. Training both of us to take over the throne, knowing you would eventually renounce your seat." His voice is shaky. "Am I really prepared to take over the throne? Who in their right mind would give me the keys to the nation?"

I turn, crossing my legs and facing him.

"I believe in you. It's not like you're going to take the throne tomorrow. It'll be years. You can learn from Mum. We've been in this family for years. It's not like you won't know what to do. You'll always have me in your court." I look down at our joined hands.

"Ellie. I'm sorry for how I acted when you came home. I was upset and hurt that you left. Even though I said to go, I was jealous that you wanted something badly enough to go after it."

I look up at his tear-filled eyes and pull him in for a big hug.

"I'm sorry too. For dropping an entire kingdom on you. For not being able to handle this life. For wanting something different. No matter where I go, I'll always love you and always be in your corner." We're both crying, sitting on the wet ground in the quickly darkening London sky. Not a prince and princess. But two siblings lamenting their loss and accepting what the future will hold.

"C'mon. I'm cold and need a drink. And you need to tell me all about this Sean. I can't have you running off for just any old guy. I need to approve."

I give him a wet smile before standing and helping him up, and we walk back to the cars. The Peter Pan statue is no longer a symbol of an impending adulthood I don't want but something that I have to fight for. With everything I have.

———

"WHAT DO YOU MEAN, you are renouncing your place in line?" My mother's voice is even, but her face betrays her confusion. "Please, give us the room." With a wave of her hand, she dismisses her staff.

"I'm sure I didn't hear you correctly. You cannot give up your place in succession of the throne." The tight line of her lips tells me she heard me perfectly.

"I meant exactly what I said. These last few weeks have shown me that I am not capable of ruling this country the way Granddad did."

"No one expects you to run the country like Dad. He was one of a kind. You have to make your own mark on the throne. It takes time to learn."

"I've been learning this my whole damn life!" The

sharp snap of my voice shocks even me. "I am not cut out for this life."

"You are born into this life. It will be the great privilege of your life to be able to lead this country with dignity and grace."

"But I don't want to!" Rising from the chair, I start pacing the room. It's warm in here for a spring day. It makes it harder to breathe. The heavy sweater I put on earlier is doing nothing to help.

"You are acting like a petulant child. I do not have time for this." She starts shuffling the papers on her desk in an attempt to dismiss me. I will not take this lying down.

"Make time. I'm your daughter, not some staff member you can easily dismiss."

"Eleanor, I've heard enough. Show me some respect and stop this conversation right now."

"I'm showing you respect by telling you of my plans. I don't plan on changing my mind."

"You should not make snap decisions at a time during great upheaval in your life. I promise you will feel better in a few weeks once things have settled down." She has gone back to the papers on her desk. My temper is boiling because she is not taking me seriously.

"This isn't some snap decision, Mum!" The room starts to spin, but I keep talking. "My entire adult life has been spent being picked apart by the media. One hair out of place, one word out of line, and I'm dragged through the mud. I cannot handle the pres—" Black spots mark my vision as I start to sway, catching the velvet couch before the world goes dark.

———

"ELEANOR. THANK HEAVENS, ARE YOU ALRIGHT?" Mum's face is above mine as the world starts to come back into focus.

"What happened?" I try to sit up, but a hand to my shoulder keeps me horizontal.

"You fainted. You were ranting and then you went ghostly white and fainted. Thankfully you didn't hurt yourself." Her face is full of concern, as her hand strokes my hair in a soothing manner.

"I'm sorry to worry you." This time I sit up, turning my head in shame that I fainted while trying to show my mum that I want to live a normal life. If I can't even take care of myself, why would she ever see me having the strength to make such a life-altering decision?

"Oh Ellie, my darling girl. It is I who should be sorry. I have never truly seen the pressure you are under. Or maybe I just didn't want to see it."

Her hands are warm on my face as she keeps my gaze on her. Mum has always made time for Jamie and me. Being raised in the royal light was not normal. We were being paraded in front of people for as long as I can remember. But if we needed her for a scraped knee or a cut, she was there. Just like she is now.

"I can no longer take my role." My voice is quiet. I try to hold back the tears, but they start leaking out. "These last few weeks have shown me what I truly desire in life. To wake up with someone I love. Work at a job I love. And at the end of the day, come home to a family I love. Without the media tearing me down at every turn."

"Is this truly what you want?" She swipes my tears away as I look at her. Instead of confusion, her face is full of concern. "This isn't something you can come back from."

I think of Sean. Of the short time we spent together

that meant everything to me. I don't know where he is or what he is doing. I don't even know if he would want me back in his life after lying about who I am. But even if he won't take me back, I know this is what I want.

"This is what I want. Truly. I know you may not understand it, but I want a simple life."

"I don't know why anyone would give this up, but she has my support." Jamie's voice echoes throughout the quiet room as he joins us on the couch, pulling me in for a hug.

"She's discussed this with you, Jamie?" She's looking at both of us with glassy eyes.

"She has. I admit, I haven't always been the best support for her, but I'm ready to step up." His voice is steady. He gives me a squeeze before turning to our mother and addressing her. "I know I haven't taken my position seriously. But I will try. I know you will be under a microscope this year before the coronation, and I promise I will change."

"James. While I don't agree with you on some things, your lively personality will be a great strength for you. I want you to stay true to yourself because the country will be lucky to have you."

A very unprincess-like snort escapes. "You might want to tone down the visits to the clubs."

"There are some things I don't need to know about my children. It's why I don't read the news, but I'm afraid it's made me short-sighted where you two are concerned. I'm sorry if I haven't been there for you."

"If you're there for us, I can't claim I have mummy-issues when I'm trying to find a woman to take all this on." Jamie waves his hand around to indicate the reality of our life.

"Jamie! For fuck's sake, Mum does not need to know about how you spend your free time!" I shove Jamie away from me. But his antics have brought a much-needed smile to my face.

"She just said she wanted to be more involved in our lives. Someone has to keep her updated since you'll be running away."

"James. Keep me updated to a point. I do not need to know everything, darling. And as for you, Eleanor," she starts, her voice back to being quiet as she pulls me towards her, "I expect you at family dinners and holidays."

"Oh Mum," I say, as a sob escapes. She wraps her arms around me as a weight lifts from my chest. I don't know what the future holds, but right now, support radiates from both my mum and Jamie. It will be a hard few months, with transitioning out and becoming a private citizen, but I know it's a decision I won't regret. No matter what happens next, I'm finally ready and open to taking whatever the future may bring.

Chapter Twenty-Three

ELLIE - FOUR WEEKS LATER

Breaking News from British News Network

In a stunning turn of events, Buckingham Palace has released a statement that Princess Eleanor will be renouncing her place in the royal line. With the passing of King Edward earlier this spring, she was set to be first in line once Princess Katherine is formally crowned early next year. We will follow this breaking story and talk to royal insiders about the preparedness of Prince James for his new role in the royal line.

"Are you going to stand out here all day?" Pierce's voice jolts me from my morose thoughts. I've been watching people come and go all morning, working up the courage to talk to Sean.

It's been a long couple of weeks, untangling myself from the threads of royal life. Figuring out what would happen with my patronages, funds, and housing was all more confusing than I care to admit. But I finally found my own place, on a gated street, that I can call my own.

"You going to come inside?" Pierce's voice is hard, harder than I've ever heard it. Iciness spreads through me at the thought of how angry his brother is.

"If it's okay."

"Of course it is, Kat. Wait, can I even call you that?"

"Ellie. You can call me Ellie." The buzzing of tattoo guns brings a smile to my face. My eyes search out Sean, but he's nowhere to be seen.

"Well, well, well. What do we have here?" Trevor stands, crossing his arms. I didn't expect anything less, but it's hard. My heart is ready to beat out of my chest. My skin is tight with anxiety.

I throw my hands up. "I come in peace. I…" I start, my voice breaking. "I was hoping to talk to Sean."

"He's not here." Trevor goes back to what he's doing, as Pierce motions for me to follow him back to the office.

"Hey, Kat." I turn to face Trevor. "Ruby misses you. Now that you're a commoner like us, come by for Sunday lunch."

I fight the tears that threaten.

"She's the next person I'll see." After everything that happened, I thought I would have lost these people. The kindness they're showing me, even though they're upset with me, reinforces the decision I made, no matter how painful it's been.

"So, any big news to share?" I close the door behind me, as Pierce takes the seat that Sean usually occupied. It doesn't fit him.

"Oh, nothing too much. Just giving up the crown, no big deal."

"And why'd you give up the throne, Ellie?" He emphasizes my name. He's not used to calling me that.

"Because I was miserable. Because up until a few months ago, I was merely existing, not living. And then I ran away. I came here and discovered everything that was missing from my life. A purpose. Friendship." I swallow back the tears that blur my vision as I make my case. "I found love."

"It's about damn time!" Pierce sweeps me into a huge hug. "He's been a miserable old sod without you."

"He has?" All the air leaves my lungs as I tighten my grip on Pierce. I never thought I'd be so welcomed back by him after what I did to his brother. But that person isn't here.

"Where is he?" I pull back, my gaze swinging around the empty office. As if by sheer force of my will, Sean might materialize in front of my eyes. "May I speak with him?"

Pierce just laughs. "We're all bloody idiots. How none of us realized you were the princess with your formal tone, I'll never know. But Sean's not here, Pink."

The nickname is exactly what I needed to hear to calm my raging nerves. "Where is he?"

"He might've had a nervous breakdown."

"He what?!" I shout, not meaning to. "I'm sorry, but is he okay? I need to see him at once."

"You know you're not a princess anymore, right? This 'at once' business has to go," he says on a laugh.

"Pierce. Where is Sean?" Any patience I have is wearing thin.

"He left. He couldn't take being here and seeing how sad you were, so he went to stay with our granddad."

My heart pangs at the mention of their granddad. Sean mentioned him a few times and held him in such regard. He still has his, while I lost mine. It still hurts.

185

"Sorry, Ellie. I didn't think. But Sean's been stateside the last few weeks."

Grabbing his arms, I pull Pierce in front of me. "This is very important. I need to see him. This can't be done over the phone."

"You'd fly to Idaho to see him?"

I smack him upside the head. "Of course I would! I fell in love with him, and I have to see if we have a chance. I have no idea if he'll take me back, but I have to try. He's it for me, Pierce. So yes, I have to go see him. Please."

He pulls out a sheet of paper and starts writing something down, before handing me an address. He pulls back before it's in my grasp. "I only ask for one thing in return."

Of course he wants something. "And what might that be?"

"That I'm there when you meet Mum. She's going to lose her shit when she finds out Sean fell in love with the princess."

———

I'M TAKING PERHAPS the biggest risk of my life. Well, perhaps the second biggest after giving up my claim to the crown. I was prepared to work much harder to win Pierce over. He was an easy target. After promising to bring Sean home, I booked the first ticket out of Heathrow.

The cool, summer air hits me as I exit the car in front of the large ranch home. After spending the last eighteen hours traveling, it feels good to be outside, stretching my legs. In all my travels, I can't remember the last time I came somewhere so remote. Dixon, Idaho is a small town that took countless hours to get to. The family farm was even farther outside the small town.

Gulping in lungfuls of clean air, I'm hit with the stark

contrast of the open skies versus the congestion of London. I wouldn't trade the busy metropolis for anything, but it's calm and peaceful here. I can see why Sean loved coming here growing up.

"Ma'am, can I help you?" A deep, booming voice comes from the front porch, thick with a country accent. The two-story house behind him looms large. It looks like a vintage log cabin, straight out of a magazine with a wrap-around porch and deep green shutters. The view of the mountains in the distance makes it look postcard ready. It's breathtaking.

"Hello, hi. I'm looking for Sean." My voice is scratchy after flying.

"You sound like you've come a long way. Come on inside. I'll see if I can track him down." His voice is warm, like hot chocolate on a cold day. It instantly puts me at ease.

"Thank you, I appreciate it. Are you Sean's grand-dad?" He holds the door open for me, nodding as I'm hit with the smell of pine. The large lobby has an empty fire-place and a bar with a few lingering guests.

"Can I get you something to drink?" The moustache tickling his upper lip makes him look even more kind with his glittering blue eyes. Eyes that mirror Sean's.

"If you have a glass of white wine, I'd love one. I'm Ellie, by the way." I extend my hand to him.

"Thomas. You're Seany's girl?" The calluses on his hands give away years of hard work. A shy smile flirts across my lips.

"I hope, but I don't know. It's been a difficult few weeks." I take the glass of wine he passes to me, taking a large gulp. To say the last few weeks have been difficult is a gross understatement. The blowback from renouncing my title was swift and cutting. I didn't leave my place for days

187

because of the media. But thankfully, Mum and Dad had an overseas tour scheduled and took the heat off me.

"Sean keeps it close to the vest. He filled me in somewhat. So, what are you doing here, princess?" His voice is full of mirth.

"No longer a princess. For once, my future is mine. And I'm here to see if maybe there's a place for Sean in it." It is still weird to say I'm no longer a princess. Maybe the more I say it, the easier it will get.

"I am sorry to hear about your grandfather. It's never easy losing a loved one." My hand instinctively goes to the flower necklace he once gave me. It still hurts to think about him. Losing him wasn't easy, but I'll always carry him with me.

"Thank you. It's been hard, but I'm carrying on."

He smacks his lips, taking a large gulp of beer. "How very British of you."

"Stiff upper lip, if you will." I give him a wink as we continue our conversation. Thomas puts me at ease. The entire flight over here, my stomach was a ball of nerves. I still have no idea what I'm doing, but I'm hoping Sean will be happy to see me.

———

SEAN

"GEMMA, I'm telling you. This car is shot. It'll break down on you again. You need a new one."

"Just fix it. I'll deal with it later." My cousin huffs, turning on her heel and stalking off to the main house. My mum's family all stayed close, living on the large property here in Dixon. Each grandkid has a cottage on the property, but some live in town. It's been the perfect escape these last few weeks. I haven't seen them in a long time, so getting to see all of them at once was just what I needed.

The place is quiet this time of day. Most guests are still coming back from the parks or taking in the sunset. Being here, in the shadow of the mountains, I feel calm. The hustle of London did nothing to help ease the ache in my heart. But when I stepped foot off the plane and saw my grandpa standing there waiting for me, I knew I had made the right decision.

His stern face cracked me within seconds and I told him everything. We had a glass of scotch at the main house, and I slept for ages, waking the following afternoon, feeling more relaxed and calmer than I had in ages.

I throw down the rag, giving up on Gemma's car for the day. My grandpa taught me car repair when I spent my summers here. I always loved spending the time with him. I appreciate it even more now knowing what Kat is going through. Or Eleanor. Or whatever she is calling herself these days.

Stretching to put the tools away, my hand idly traces the new tattoo on my bicep. Normally a piece this big would be done in stages, but I had Pierce go straight through, needing the pain as a distraction from the pain in my chest.

All I want is to grab a cold beer and then go relax in the small house my grandpa had ready for me. As I push open the door to the main house, the open windows pull in the evening breeze. It never feels this good in London. Gemma's back behind the counter, her eyes wide. I look at her, confused, until I look past her to the bar. Sitting there, with my grandpa, is Kat. Her hair is back to that vibrant pink I loved so much.

I still have a visceral reaction to seeing Kat. Everything

about her turns me on, yet I don't understand what she's doing here. Why she's not off learning the ropes to become the future monarch.

"Hi, Sean." Her voice is soft. Quiet. She looks tired, like she hasn't slept in weeks.

"What the hell are you doing here?" The question bursts out of me before I can stop it. My grandpa leaves the bar, slapping me on the back of the head as he goes.

"That's no way to talk to a lady, son. Now go talk to her and hear what she has to say." He gives me a small shove in Kat's direction.

"Is there somewhere more private we can talk?" Kat asks, looking over my shoulder. Gemma is openly staring at the two of us. No doubt she is enthralled that Kat is here.

"Follow me." I head back out the door I had entered, holding it for her. She brushes past me, and I suck in a breath. That familiar floral scent tugs at my heart. This woman burrowed her way deep into my heart and didn't let go. Even when shit hit the fan.

We walk the short distance to my place, and I allow her to go inside. Her gaze sweeps over the tiny kitchen and living room. It's small, but cozy.

"Sean—" she starts, but I cut her off.

"I don't even know what to call you. Kat? Eleanor?" After everything that went down, I couldn't help the hurt at not knowing who she really was. I took that pain out with the tattoo that was the very essence of this woman in front of me.

"Eleanor. Ellie Ainsworth. Former Princess of the United Kingdom. It's a pleasure to make your acquaintance."

Damn, if she still doesn't have a regal air about her. I take her extended hand, and a spark of electricity shoots up my arm. Christ, the effect this woman still has on me.

Even running away, I can't escape it. Maybe I don't want to escape it.

It takes a minute for my brain to grab on to what she said.

"Wait, former princess?" I try not to think about how good she looks standing here with me. She may sound regal, but right now, she's every bit my pink-haired goddess.

"You haven't been watching the news?"

"Why would I be watching the news?"

She shakes her head at me. "Well, something kind of big happened. I only assumed you'd hear about it. I gave up the throne."

Holy shit. She gave up the throne? A shock like I've never known rolls through me. Was she even allowed to give up the crown? Was she running away again? My head was spinning. "Are you even allowed to do that?"

"I can. And I did." She's smiling. A smile that I know is only for me.

"Is this a joke?" Her face falls. She crosses her arms in front of her.

"It's not a joke. After my granddad passed away, we each got a letter from him. Mine told me to follow my heart. That it was okay if I didn't want the throne. I suspect he always knew. So I gave up my claim to the crown and am now a private citizen."

"Wow." No words come to mind. I try to speak, but just open and close my mouth, gaping like a fish. I can't wrap my head around this revelation.

"I came here because I want to see if we still have a chance. I know I hurt you when I didn't tell you who I was, but I love you, Sean. It was never a game. Never a bored princess wanting to play a part. You gave me a safe place when I ran, and I fell in love with you." She takes a few tentative steps towards me.

"I know it may take some time to get back to where we were, but I want you. I want to live a quiet life with you. Wake up next to you. Find a job where I can make a difference. And come home to our own place. To you. Make love every night."

I try to hide the smile, but I can't. Her version of our life sounds pretty damn good. I take a few steps forward. My hands rest on her hips, turning her so I can lift her onto the counter. I want her more than I want my next breath. I crave her with a bone deep ache in my soul. The love I have for her is a once-in-a-lifetime feeling. Ellie is it for me.

"We'll have a lot to figure out. I can't imagine they'd just let you go quietly." I rest my forehead against hers. Her hands tentatively rest on my chest, not knowing where to go. It's so unlike my feisty girl from a few weeks back.

"Security will be an issue, but we'll have that for some time until we can figure out a better plan. I'm hoping you still might need a receptionist because I'm kind of unemployed now." She lets out a small laugh. God, all I want is to kiss those lips of hers. Having her here reminds me of how much I missed her these last few weeks.

I wrap my arms around her waist, pulling her closer to me. "Ellie. I won't lie. It hurt when you didn't tell me who you really were, but I get it. You're the fucking princess. Or were, I should say. But being here, talking with my grandpa, made me realize I do love you. And it killed me because I thought I was going to have to let you go. I mean, what right does a half-British, half-American tattoo artist have to the princess?"

Ellie's hands cup my cheeks. Firm. This time, knowing exactly where they belong. "You are the only person who ever saw me for me. The only man I've ever loved. You have every right to me. To my body. To my heart. No one else."

Passion and love blaze in those deep eyes. Eyes I've missed. Lips I've missed kissing. My lips crush hers. Tasting her. Claiming her. She opens immediately, and I sweep my tongue in and groan at the taste of her I've missed so much. Her hands scrape the nape of my neck. I pull her closer to me. Not a breath of air between our bodies. Our tongues clash, fighting for control, neither one of us ready to relinquish to the other. She pulls back first, her lips swollen.

"So, what do you say, Sean? Want to take on a jobless, ex-princess with no idea what she wants to do with her life?"

"Are you ready to take on a tattoo artist who will do nothing but support you and love you and walk next to you while you figure out your life?"

"Oh Sean." Her voice breaks as she pulls me back into her. Soft gasps escape as she clutches me tightly to her, no doubt releasing all the pent-up emotions from the last few weeks.

All I can do is hold her. Hold on and never let go.

"How are you doing, Ellie?" The name rolls out easier than I thought.

She gives me a watery smile. "You know what the worst part is?" I shake my head. "The money is changing."

"The money is changing?" I'm confused. She must read that confusion, because she continues.

"Growing up, Granddad would always sneak us a ten-pound note. 'So you don't forget my face.' And now, they are already changing the money. And I'm so worried I'll forget his face."

Tears stream down her cheeks as I pull her back into

my chest. Her hands wrap around my arms. My shirt sleeve rides up, exposing my new ink.

"Sean." Her fingers cover her lips as she takes in the matching tattoo on my bicep. It's the same wildflowers she has on her side, just more to cover the space. She doesn't touch it, but stares. "You got this for me?"

"I was angry and upset. But I never stopped loving you." I drop my forehead to hers. "I always said I needed to find something I wanted enough to put there. Turns out, it was you."

"It's beautiful. I can't believe after all this time, this is what you got tattooed here." Her eyes watch her fingers as she traces the pattern. I pull her hand away, kissing each finger.

"I love it, Sean." Her lips are on mine again. A deep, soul-affirming kiss. My hands go to pull her shirt and bra off. The bright ink on her side is a reminder that our time in London was real and beautiful. I have to have her right now.

"Just so you know, no one is ever allowed to ink you." I trace the pattern on her side, brushing the underside of her breasts. "Only me. No one else gets to touch you."

"Only you," she whispers. I lift her off the counter and carry her to the bed, lying down with her on top of me. Her lips are a hot brand as they move over my skin. My hands move to the button and zipper on her jeans, before moving to cup her ass, rocking her into me. The need and friction grow between us. Before I can make a move, she's off me. She's biting her bottom lip, eyes roving over my body. My dick tents my pants. She slowly wiggles out of her jeans and underwear. This woman I love with everything I have is here. I can't believe it. I stand and wrap my arms around her, leaning her against the wall and biting down on her shoulder. My fingers skate down her skin, her bare pussy slick and ready for me. She gasps as I easily slide a finger in. Her hand flies to my neck, holding on for dear life.

"God, I've missed this. How you know me so well." Her voice is husky, dripping with need. I lick back up to her ear, sucking her earlobe into my mouth, nibbling down.

"No one knows you like I do. And no one ever will." I continue working my finger in and out of her. Adding another, then a third. Her pussy is a vise every time I drive back in.

"Oh, God! I'm..." She doesn't finish her statement as her body shakes with pleasure. Her orgasm races through her. Her inner walls pulse on my fingers, my hand now sticky with her release. Ellie's body is limp in mine. I forgot how much I love when she's blissed out like this.

Not wasting any time, I shuck my jeans and boxer briefs off. Using her wetness to stroke my dick, her beautiful naked body makes me painfully hard.

"Are you ready for me?" I carry us back over to the bed. With all the care in the world, I set her in the middle of the comforter. My hands brush the pink hair from her face.

"Sean. I need you now." Her fingers are caressing my face as she pulls my lips down to hers. A moment passes between us. There's no need for protection as I slide through her slick folds, finding heaven once again.

"Fuck, Ellie." Her slick pussy engulfing my dick is almost too much. Her warmth surrounds me in the best way. Looking down at where our bodies meet, I start to move, thrusting in and out of her in a devastating pace.

"God, I've missed this." The muffled sound of her voice rings out as I thrust in and out of her. My own orgasm is building. My balls screw up tight, ready for release. My spine tingles as I feel her start to lose it. Her pussy suffocates my dick as she screams. "Yes!" The shout pushes me over the edge.

"Ellie. Fuck, Ellie. Yes!" I say her name over and over. I can't get enough of her. I never want to leave this perfect heaven we're in.

"That was the best fucking thing in my life." I feel her smile against me.

Falling to her side, I wrap my body around hers. I've missed her curves. Missed falling asleep with her and waking up with her by my side.

"I still can't believe you're here." I brush a few stray hairs from her forehead. "And you went back to pink."

She smiles. Her face fills with love for me. The best fucking thing in the world. "Don't they say pinks have more fun?" The touch of her fingers on my tattoos is a balm I didn't know I needed. "It took me too long to get here, but there was a lot to sort out."

"How did everyone react? How's your brother doing with all this?"

Her eyes briefly close, filled with guilt. "It wasn't as much of a shock to him as I would've thought. We've both been doing this our entire lives, and now his timeline just got moved up. I worry about him handling it, but my granddad gave me the courage to do it."

"I wish I could've met him. Not the king, but the man. He sounds wonderful." Those deep blue eyes get glassy. I pull her tighter into my arms, dropping a kiss onto the top of her head.

"He would've loved you. It's been a rough few weeks, but I'm hoping now it'll be easier." Her breath ghosts my chest.

"What's the plan?"

"Stay here in bed with you. Make up for lost orgasms."

She kisses my pec, tracing her fingers up and down the ridges of my abs.

"As wonderful as that sounds, and I'm not disagreeing, seems like we still have a lot to figure out." I run my hand up and down her arm, hoping the answer will come to us. She sits up, swinging her leg over me to straddle me. Her hands land on my chest, absently tracing the tattoos there.

"We could stay here for a little while. Let the chaos in London die down a bit. I don't really know what the future holds now, but I just want to be with you. Have a family. I don't care where."

"Jumping pretty far ahead there, aren't we?" I smirk at her, but she just beams down at me. My heart stops in my chest at how much I love this woman.

"I realized how much I wanted a family, kids, with you. I was always so opposed to the idea because it was forced upon me. All that 'heir and the spare' business. But having your kids? Give me a dozen."

I sit up. Our naked chests brush together, her arms wrapping around my shoulders. "You really want to have kids?"

She nods her head, biting on her lip. Fuck if that doesn't make my dick twitch. She feels it because she grinds herself on my lap. I flip us over, settling back on top of her.

"Better get started then."

Epilogue

SEAN - NINE MONTHS LATER

"Ellie! Car's here. We need to get going." Fiddling with the cuffs on my shirt, I glance at the clock to see we need to leave now if we're to be on time. All week, the stress of today has been coming off Ellie in waves. I know she doesn't want to be in the spotlight, especially now, but it's a big day. Coronation Day.

"Coming, love. I forgot how long it takes to get royal ready." Her sweet voice carries down the stairs as I wait for her. I never thought we'd get to live this life together. When I found out who she was, I thought we were over, that there was no future for a princess and a tattoo artist. But she gave it all up for her own future. For me. And now, our life was going to be even better.

"What do you think?" Her voice draws me out of my own head. She always steals my breath with her beauty, but damn if she isn't gorgeous in the most elaborate dress I've ever seen.

"You look fecking incredible." I pull her to me, capturing her lips with mine in a sweet kiss.

"They did some good work. You can't see a thing." She

steps out of my hold, turning to her side. Whoever made this dress did a damn good job at hiding our secret.

"I'm glad we get to keep the little one to ourselves for just a little while longer." I rub my hands over her stomach. She's got the barest hint of a bump, but with all the material of this dress, you'd have no idea.

"It would cause quite the scandal if the press could see me now." Ellie's voice is quiet, and she tucks her hands over mine.

"I don't give a shite about any of them. It's you and me, love. Always us." I turn her head and capture her lips in a deeper kiss. Her little remark tells me just how nervous she is about today. Thankfully she isn't hounded by the media like she used to be. For a few weeks when we returned to London, she was hounded daily. There's still some paparazzi, but it's not as bad as it could be. Thank God.

A sharp rap on the door breaks us apart. "Just a few hours and then we'll be home."

"Promise?" she asks quietly.

"Promise."

———

Ellie

"YOU THINK this will actually start on time?" Sean's warm hand on mine is the only thing keeping me grounded. The amount of material on my dress floating down in layers is astounding. While it hides the small bump I have, it's extremely warm in the packed abbey.

"We can only hope." At that precise moment, horns

start trumpeting outside. "Looks like you must be good luck."

The sound of thousands of people rising echoes throughout the grand hall. "Here we go," Sean mumbles beside me. Taking a deep breath, we rise with the rest of the crowd, awaiting my mum's grand entrance.

What seems like hours later, she finally makes her appearance. The Coronation Robes are held by my father, brother, Charlotte, and my uncle. The jewels on her crown gleam brighter than I've ever seen them. My mother is the perfect queen. There is no one more fit to lead our country than she.

As she takes her place front and center, Jamie takes his place beside me.

"Doing alright, Ellie?"

My voice gets caught in my throat, so I can only manage a nod. He pulls me into a quick side hug, my other hand holding onto Sean. As the Archbishop calls for us to sit, the long ceremony begins.

Imagining myself in my mother's shoes causes my chest to tighten. The weight of the crown. The weight of the robes. It all presses down on me thinking this could have been my future. If this would have been me today, I don't know how I would be feeling. I wouldn't be ready. But my mother is the epitome of regal. Having also been taught by my grandfather, she will lead the country with all the grace and confidence I could never muster.

"Madam, is your Majesty willing to take the Oath?"

"I am willing." Her voice is strong as she accepts her oath to the crown.

———

"HOW ARE YOU FEELING, YOUR MAJESTY?" Mum comes over to our small group at the celebratory ball. She's changed into a new gown, a beautiful off-the-shoulder gown with intricate gold threads woven throughout the flowers on the dress to represent the entirety of the Commonwealth.

"Queen-like."

"Congratulations, Your Majesty." Sean leans over to greet her as our family mingles with the guests.

"Thank you. And how is everything going with the foundation?"

Sean's smile is bright. "It's going very well. I couldn't have done it without Ellie." He pulls me into his side.

"She was always good at fundraising for her charities," Mum says, laughter in her voice.

"You're both too kind. If it weren't for Sean, there would be no programme to start with. I'm just lucky I get to help out."

When we got back to London, helping Sean get the funds for his art programme was at the top of my to-do list. As a former princess, I wasn't above throwing my name around to get Sean the funds he needed. And now I split my time between the shop and the school. There's nothing I love more than being covered in paint by the time I head home for the day. And seeing Sean work with the students and share his love of art? I didn't think I could love him any more.

It's a far cry from where we are now. Being surrounded by all this pomp and circumstance makes me grateful this isn't my life anymore.

"Mind if I steal Eleanor away for a few minutes?" Mum's voice pulls me from my thoughts.

"You're the queen." Sean kisses me on the cheek before

Mum loops her arm through mine and guides me down an empty hall.

"How are you doing today, Eleanor?" The long hall is quiet as we leave the noise of the ball behind us.

"Shouldn't I be asking you that?" I turn to look at her, but her concern is only for me.

"This was something I've been preparing for my entire life. I learned from the best." She goes quiet as she remembers her beloved father. "I was ready."

"You did beautifully. I couldn't be prouder." I squeeze her to me. I thought when I left the royal folds, I would feel a disconnect from my family. But instead, it's only brought us closer together.

"Thank you, my darling. Now, would you like to fill me in on your little secret?" Her knowing eyes turn to me.

"What are you talking about?" I keep my voice steady, not wanting to give anything away.

"I might be the queen, but I'm still your mum, Eleanor. I know you're pregnant."

My hands instinctively go to my stomach. "How can you tell?"

Her hands cup my face and bring my eyes to hers. They are glassy with emotion. "You are practically glowing. And Sean has barely let you out of his sight all morning," she says on a laugh.

"I can't get him to give me breathing room. He thinks I'm going to break," I say with an eye roll.

"Did I ever tell you how your dad treated me when I was pregnant with you and James?" I shake my head in response. "God love him, he followed me around everywhere. Had water or different shoes or a change of clothes if I was hot or cold. Couldn't breathe without him being on top of me."

"I can't even imagine. That will probably be Sean the

entire time." My eyes drift down to my hand, which is rubbing my stomach.

"I'm sure he'll calm down once things progress further. Or until you put him in his place."

"Yes, that will happen. I'm pregnant, not fragile." I give her a quick glance, before looking back down. "You're not mad I didn't tell you?"

"Oh darling, no. I know the worry of not telling people until you're past a certain point. I can't believe that I get to be a grandmum." Her smile is so bright, it's infectious.

"I can't wait to be a mum. I'm so happy, and I love the life I have. The life Sean and I created. There's nothing I wanted more in life, and I finally have it."

"I know I didn't always understand why you wanted to leave, but you have carved out a beautiful life for yourself, Eleanor, and I couldn't be prouder."

My vision blurs as tears cloud my eyes. On a day that is supposed to be all about the queen, she's being my mum first and foremost. Wrapping my arms around her as best I can with the large gowns we're wearing, I squeeze her tight to me. Mother and daughter. Not the queen and a former princess. I won't remember the pageantry when I think back on this day. I will cherish this moment between the two of us.

"Mum! Ellie! Where are you two?" Jamie's voice carries down the hall, breaking apart our moment.

"Right here, James." Mum takes my hand as we walk over to meet him.

"You're not supposed to disappear. You're the woman of the hour," Jamie says, swinging his arm over Mum's shoulders.

"I'm the queen. I can do what I please."

"Can I use that excuse? That sounds bloody brilliant."

"You're not the king." Mum's stern gaze turns to him.

"Thank God. I'm not ready for you to be our king yet," I say on a laugh.

As we return to the ballroom, Sean is standing on the outside, looking in at all the dignitaries still partying the night away. Butterflies still flutter in my stomach every time I see him. Just a short year ago, I never thought I would find my happily ever after. The path my mother is so eloquently following in today was my destiny.

Sean's eyes swing in my direction, and it pulls me into his orbit. God, I love this man and the life we've created together.

"Ready to go home, love?"

"Yes."

As for this princess? She finally got her happily ever after.

The End

Want to find out more about Sean and Ellie's life in London? Signup for my newsletter for an exclusive bonus epilogue!

Join my Facebook Reader's group, Emily Silver's Travelers, to stay in the know about all future books!

Thank you so much for reading Royal Reckoning! If you enjoyed it, you can leave a review here.

James' book is up next! Read on for a sneak peek!

Sneak Peek

JAMES

"Can you think with anything besides your prick, James?" Bloody hell, I'm in for it now. I can't help it if the paparazzi are leaking old photos of me. Even if this one is awful. I'm getting sucked off in a club. You can't see anything inappropriate, but anyone with half a brain knows what's going on.

"The Queen will be over to have a word with you shortly. This is out of my hands." For fuck's sake. It's never good when the Queen has to get involved.

"I'll be sure to let her know it won't happen again."

My advisor, Charles, gives me an appraising look. His bushy white eyebrows are furrowed. I'm sure I've given him wrinkles early in life. I can't help it if I like to have fun.

"Will it, though? This isn't the first time we've seen this happen, and I doubt it will be the last. You're first in line to the throne now. This behaviour is unbecoming of the future King."

"You don't need to remind me of my position in life." My voice is harsh as I snap back at him. Ever since my twin renounced her spot in the royal line, all eyes have

207

been on me. Before, my behaviour was considered cute. That of a playboy prince sowing his oats. Now, everyone has turned on me.

"Someone needs to." That voice sends people scurrying to stand and bow. It's still strange seeing Mum as the Queen. I stand, buttoning my blazer as I do. "You all can leave. I'd like a moment with my son."

My advisor and his staff exit on a bow. Cowards. Leaving me here to fend for myself. Heading to the tea cart, I pour us each a cuppa.

"Thank you, darling."

I take a sip, eyeing her with suspicion. "To what do I owe the pleasure of this visit, Mum?"

"As if you don't already know." She sits on the velvet loveseat in my office. Everything here is velvet. Quite annoying really, considering I'm the future King and it's decorated for an old grandmum.

"Why don't you enlighten me?" I can't help the cheekiness in my voice.

Mum sets her cup down on the coffee table in a huff. "James, this has to stop. You are almost thirty now. You can't keep expecting people to excuse this behaviour."

"It's amazing how quickly they turned on me."

She pinches the bridge of her nose. Mum's hair was always a dark brown like mine, but now there's more grey peppered in. It gives her a regal air. But today, it's just pissing me off.

"If you don't start making some changes, and soon, I'll be forced to take action."

"You'll be forced to take action? What the bloody hell does that even mean?" My voice carries as I push off the loveseat. "I don't need you controlling my life." Shoving my hands through my hair, I try to take a calming breath.

"You have yet to prove to me that you are capable of

taking on even the smallest of duties that I was doing for your grandfather when I was your age. You are just not ready to be King." Her voice becomes quiet as she mentions him. He died almost a year ago, but it still hurts to think about him. He was one of the best Kings England has ever seen, and I know Mum is doing everything in her power to live up to his standard.

"Maybe if you'd actually give me those duties to do, I could try. Have you ever thought of that?" My hands on my hips, I stare Mum down. I hate being questioned like this. "I'm already being held to an impossible standard."

I know I've hit a sore spot when Mum rolls her eyes. "An impossible standard? You were allowed to run around with no regard to the crown and get away with it. Your sister was held to an impossible standard and look where that got us."

"That was below the belt." Ellie hated everything about royal life. The media. The people commenting on her every move and appearance. She's much happier living as a private citizen, but damn, if that doesn't hurt.

"It's true. You need to be held accountable, James. And it's going to start right now." She pushes off of her seat and goes to leave.

"What do you mean 'it's going to start right now'?"

"I am not getting any younger, James. This position has a way of aging you before you're ready. Dad did everything he could to prepare Eleanor for the crown, but now, I'm afraid I must do the same for you."

"Mum. I'll do better. I promise."

She opens the door to leave. "Until you show me that, then I'll continue with my own plans."

Fucking hell.

The music is too loud tonight. Club Mayfair has always been my favourite. I get special treatment here. All the free drinks, sexy women fawning all over me, and no press allowed inside. The scotch is doing little to quell my nerves. A blonde is sitting by my side, her dangerously long nails trailing up and down my thigh. It's doing little to arouse me tonight.

I'd be all for a quick romp in the sack with her, but right now, Mum's words keep playing on a loop in my head.

Not ready to be King.

How does one even prepare to be King? It's not like I haven't been paying attention all these years. Sure, I've been more concerned with women, but I still know what it takes to run a country. Or at least I think I do.

"You want to get out of here, Prince James?" Any attraction I might have had to this woman goes down the toilet at those last two words. I know most women are with me because of who I am, but I can't handle it tonight.

"Sorry…" Bloody hell, I can't even remember her name. "I'm just not feeling it tonight."

I nod to my Personal Protection Officers, my PPOs, that I'm ready to leave. It's still early, so hopefully I can pop over and see the one person who might actually be able to talk some sense into me.

"Are we heading home, Your Highness?" my security officer asks, as I dodge the questions of the paparazzi that are awaiting my exit before getting in the idling car.

"Head to Ellie's, please." I throw my blazer over the backseat and close my eyes. Why is this shite bothering me even more today? Maybe because it's coming from Mum. It's my advisors who are the ones to condemn me for my behaviour. Never has Mum gotten involved before.

"Shall I call ahead and let her know that we are coming?"

"Please do. Otherwise, she may be irritated."

The car lurches into the street as the noise of the club fades away. I'm hoping my sister will be a voice of reason. For being this early in the evening, it's a quick drive through the city. When we pass through the gated entry of Ellie's neighbourhood, I release a breath.

"Thanks, guys. I won't be long." I hop out of the car, seeing Ellie at the front door. Her once brown hair is now pink, a stark contrast to mine.

"Why the hell are you coming over to my place at nine at night when you could be out at the clubs?" She waves me in as I kiss her cheek.

"No Sean tonight?" My sister's face softens at the mention of her partner, Sean. If she hadn't stumbled into his tattoo parlour when she ran away from the palace, I don't know where I'd be right now. That's a slippery slope to go down.

"He had a session run late. What's brought you over here?"

I flop down on her couch, rubbing my eyes. "Mum. The palace. You name it."

She messes around in the kitchen before returning to the living room. "I'm guessing it has to do with that picture that is spread all over the news?" She hands me a scotch before sitting in a chair next to me.

"You saw it too?" Christ, I didn't think she'd be looking at tabloids once she left the royal life behind.

"It's hard not to hear it from the parents when they're whispering about me at the school." Ellie took the reins of Sean's after school art programme and helped build it into what it is today. She keeps it running on the days that Sean is at his tattoo parlour. I don't know how they manage both, but they love it.

"Hopefully you didn't see it." I shiver, taking a long pull of the scotch.

"Absolutely not! I wouldn't go out looking for that. But it serves you right for getting caught. It's not like you were ever discreet with your women."

"Thanks, Ellie. Just what I needed tonight." My eyes roll on their own.

"Why are you so morose tonight? Couldn't find anyone to take home at the club?"

"Is that really all people think I do?" Shite, maybe Mum does have a point.

"Jamie. It's all you lead people to believe. There're no photos of you going to galas or art show openings or state dinners because you're always going out with women. It takes precedence over anything else you might do."

"Fecking hell. You sound just like Mum." I shake my head. "But you may have a solid point."

"Is the world ending?" she asks on a gasp. "I don't think I've ever heard you say those words to me before."

"Alright, alright. Quit being a smart arse."

The front door opens with a bang as Sean races in. "Is everything okay in here?" He looks haggard. "Oh, hey, James. What are you doing here? I thought something happened."

"Other than me being a prick, nothing going on."

Sean walks over and drops a kiss on Ellie's head. I can't be bitter towards my sister. She was not cut out for royal life. Seeing her this happy, starting her own family, makes me realize I do need to step up and take responsibility for myself.

I gulp down the rest of my scotch and drop it on the table behind me. "Thanks, Ellie. You've been a big help."

She looks confused. "You don't have to leave now that Sean is home. Are you going to be okay?" Her voice sounds concerned. She worries about me more than she should.

"I'll be fine. You just helped me see a few things more clearly."

Ellie gives me a wary look. "If you're sure." She walks over to give me a hug as I head out.

"See you later, Sean."

"Always a pleasure, James." He waves me off as I jog down the stairs.

I just need a plan to present to Mum. Maybe she'll see reason if I start to take control of my life. As much as it pains me to admit, even cutting the club visits in half would be a good start. I may be the prince, but I'm by no means a saint.

Read Reckless Royal in Kindle Unlimited today!

Author Note

I have had this book written for months, and it just so happened to release with the passing of Prince Philip. As a lover of everything royal, I was so sad to hear of his passing. He was such a stoic leader for the United Kingdom, and his love story with Elizabeth is one for the ages. I hope we should all be so lucky to get to experience the love these two had.

To all the amazing authors out there that have supported me on this journey...YOU ARE THE BEST!! I never dreamed of the support I would receive from the romance community when I started this author dream, but romance is really where it's at! And to my Accountability Tribe... Norma and AK...you two are amazing and keep me going on the days I want to throw in the towel!

To the best beta readers...Tara, Audrey, Norma and Nicole...thank you for helping me make this book amazing! To my ARC team...you guys rock and I love having you on this journey with me!

And to all the amazing readers out there...you all have made this one hell of a journey so far, and shown me so much love that it brings me to tears some days! I can't wait to see where this year takes us together!

xo, Emily

About the Author

After winning a Young Author's Award in second grade, Emily Silver was destined to be a writer. She loves writing strong heroines and the swoony men who fall for them.

A lover of all things romance, Emily started writing books set in her favorite places around the world. As an avid traveler, she's been to all seven continents and sailed around the globe.

When she's not writing, Emily can be found sipping cocktails on her porch, reading all the romance she can get her hands on and planning her next big adventure!

Find her on social media to stay up to date on all her adventures and upcoming releases!

Also by Emily Silver

Book 1: Love in the Antarctic

Book 2: Love in Europe

Book 3: Love in Australia

Love Under an Italian Sky - Newsletter Exclusive

the
AINSWORTH
ROYALS

Book 2: Reckless Royal

Book 3: Royal Relations